The Delegation

Michael Moloney

Plassey Publishing Ltd

Published 2009
by Plassey Publishing Ltd
1

The Delegation is a work of fiction and, except in the case of historical fact, names, characters, organisations, places or events are either the product of the author's imagination or are used fictitiously. Any resemblance of fictitious characters to actual persons, living or dead, is purely coincidental.

ISBN: 978-0-9562170-0-4
A CIP record of this book is available from the British Library
First published as a paperback in Ireland in 2009
Plassey Publishing Ltd
57 Cremorne, Dublin 16, Ireland
www.plasseypublishing.ie
info@plasseypublishing.ie
Printed in Ireland by Gemini International Ltd.

My thanks to family and friends for their support and comments:

in particular to

Des Kenny, Vincent McDonnell, Lloyd Mudiwa and
Gráinne Sarsfield;

my sister, Joan Mac Kernan;

Cilian, Fiachra and Ailbhe;

and, of course, to my wife, Tríona, for everything.

Dedicated to the memory of four people who had a wonderfully
innate sense of justice

Mary and Thomas McMahon and Martha and Michael Moloney

and

to all those who work for justice.

Michael Moloney

Michael Moloney was born in Limerick in 1952.
He lives in Dublin. This is his first novel.

Prologue

Salisbury, Zimbabwe: 1980

The body bag slid from the back of the army lorry and fell to the ground with a dull thud, accompanied by a sigh of escaping air. The African soldier again grabbed the taper of one corner and dragged it across the floor of the hangar. In a swift movement, he bent his knees, gathered the sack-like weight into his arms and dumped it into a shallow crate.

'One strong silent man is better than ten who talk.'

The soldier ignored the comment from Minister Julius Charamba and hammered a nail into a corner of the lid.

'A nail in each corner is enough.'

Again without acknowledging he was being spoken to, the soldier moved around the crate, driving in each of the four nails with one blow.

'No point making it too difficult to re-open. I'm sure you have a proper coffin arranged in Dublin, so please excuse our lack of ceremony. This way also ensures that we attract the minimum of attention.'

'Yes, all arranged. I'm sure there will be quite a fuss,' was the dry reply from the Irishman.

The forklift carrying the crate disappeared through the just wide enough opening in the hangar door. Minister Julius Charamba and the Irishman followed to the exit.

'I think it's best that we take our farewells here. Let us shake hands for the last time, my Irish friend. If I can call you that.'

'Perhaps better friend than enemy.'

The crate sat among the luggage on the tarmac where the baggage handlers were already loading the plane.

'Who would have thought it would end like this? Comrade Mugabe has asked, has ordered, me to tell you that he would not have wanted this outcome. He likes you Irish, you know.'

'Maybe because he has had no quarrel with us.'

'Comrade Mugabe stressed that you should convey to his friends in Ireland that we would never have wanted an Irish citizen to die like that in the Zimbabwean struggle for freedom.'

The young man stood, head bent, pretending to examine the contents of his manila file.

'Didn't I tell you I want to get back from London on the early evening flight? What sort of timetable do you call this?'

'But Senator...'

'Noooo "buts". Do I have to spell it out for you? I ...want... to...return... from... London... on... the... early... evening... flight.' Senator Gerry Cahill threw his copy of the schedule at the junior civil servant, the sheaf of papers fanning against his chest.

'Not in the middle of the bloody night!'

John Mulligan shifted in his high-backed chair, wanting to ignore the scene at the other end of the room. Everything has a price, Mulligan thought as he studied the portrait of Lord Iveagh, the original owner of the Department of Foreign Affairs building, hanging over the fireplace. Did Cahill's acting private secretary, now on the point of tears, not know he would have to suffer this indignity until he landed back in Ireland again? What had he been offered to agree to accompany Cahill on this trip to Rhodesia? In return for suffering the bullying, young Tom Kennedy might get an early promotion. Rumour had it this was a promise given by the Department's Secretary himself to bribe someone to take the job nobody wanted. Cahill waved his hand and his private secretary left the room, avoiding eye contact with Mulligan.

'Soooo, Mr Mulligan, we're off to Africa.' Senator Cahill was in a good mood now, giving John Mulligan the benefit of the charm that had secured him the top count in his constituency in every general election, except the last one, for more than twenty years. After decades of ignoring talk of financial corruption, Cahill's constituents had turned against him after one of the UK tabloids, not bound by the niceties of Ireland's journalism, had revealed that he had fathered a child out of marriage with a woman in Dublin. The voters had finally rejected him for his lifelong hypocrisy, having

7

watched him strut to the top of the church Sunday after Sunday, his leather shoes echoing off the tiles. That, and his humiliation of his childless wife, daughter of the former leader of the local Flying Column guerrilla fighters during the War of Independence, had eventually brought about Gerry Cahill's downfall.

The two men were taking their measure. They knew each other of old. Cahill had been Minister for Foreign Affairs during Mulligan's fall from grace. He saw Mulligan as a failed civil servant with a failed marriage and a failed life. Ten years previously, when Cahill had breached protocol and publicly castigated John Mulligan for 'letting the country down', neither could have foreseen that they would be heading off to Africa together. Would it be possible to keep their mutual contempt in check for five whole days?

'We are indeed.' Mulligan added, 'Senator,' savouring Cahill's fall from ministerial status. When Mulligan heard that Cahill had been pipped for the last seat in a nail-biting election count, he had rubbed his hands in glee and whispered, 'good riddance'. But Cahill had been appointed to the Senate, a reward for his years as party henchman and fundraiser, and now, when no minister was available to lead this special mission, Cahill had got word of the difficulty and volunteered. Despite the Department Secretary's protestations, the Taoiseach himself had endorsed Cahill as delegation leader.

If he was hurt by the jibe, Cahill gave no hint of it and waited for Mulligan to continue.

'We touch down in Salisbury on Saturday morning. Everything is arranged.'

'Good.'

'At least, all the flights are. We're having trouble putting the key appointments in place. Particularly with Mugabe. But I'm told it's best to go on spec.'

'I'm sure you're right, Mr Mulligan. Let's get down there and check it out.'

Mulligan did not know if he was being sarcastic or accommodating, but Cahill was walking towards the door, saying over his shoulder, 'Get me when the Brits and the Yanks arrive.'

Gerry Cahill had the door almost closed when he put his head back into the room. 'And this time in Africa, Mr Mulligan, try and keep your fly shut.'

Cahill shut the door sharply, not even bothering to check how deeply he had cut Mulligan, left alone now in the vast room, his flaring face making his beard itchy. He got up slowly and lit a cigarette. He was only just cooling down, his cigarette almost finished, when Tom Kennedy entered the room after a deferential knock and held the door open wide for the others.

'Excuse me, Mr Mulligan, the ambassadors have arrived,' he stated formally.

'The senator has asked me to make his apologies. He has been unavoidably delayed.' After letting this lie sink in, Mulligan extended his hand to the tall, cravat-wearing British envoy: then to the already sweating, overweight American and, greeting them by their first names, to the two dark-suited officials.

'I'm sure Senator Cahill has a very busy schedule.' It was the British ambassador who spoke, acknowledging Mulligan's tact, knowing that Cahill was going to let them cool their heels.

'Indeed, Mr Mulligan, we are very pleased to speak directly with you.' The British ambassador moved his long fingers across the studs of the high-backed leather chair and added without any apparent tongue-in-cheek, 'We know you have substantial experience of, shall we say, the African scene.'

'As you can appreciate, Mr Mulligan, we have a very delicate situation on our hands. The new parliament has been sworn in and the former guerrilla leaders are making it clear that they are most unhappy with us.' He motioned towards the Americans but, before the US representative could say anything, added, 'Of course, most of their ire is aimed at Britannia, but overall there is a real danger that Mugabe will lead Rhodesia into the hands of the Soviets.'

'Mugabe is acting like a sulky teenager, Mr Mulligan,' the American ambassador interjected. 'He won't even take a phone call.' He shrugged in response to Mulligan's sympathetic nods, the jelly of his upper body creating a ripple. 'We have a man down there at the moment checking things out. One of our guys from the Nairobi embassy. He reckons Mugabe is going to cut all links. Lots of the old guard will be packing their bags soon. Including some of your Irish contacts!' He spoke quickly, brimming with information. 'So, John,' the American was getting buddy-buddy, 'we badly need you,' he stopped, apparently correcting himself, 'we need Senator Cahill to get to Mugabe and put him straight on where the future of Rhodesia lies.'

'Of course,' the British ambassador added, speaking towards the photo of the minister getting his seal of office from the president, 'we would have preferred if your excellent Minister for Foreign Affairs were available but we appreciate the exigencies of high office.'

'The senator is very enthusiastic about the visit.' Mulligan wanted to deflect from the weakness of the mission team and, despite his dislike for Cahill, was annoyed at the patronising tone.

'We reckon Senator Cahill has his reasons.' The American official spoke from the end of the room, but when Mulligan glanced at him in surprise he was unwilling to elaborate.

The door swung open and Cahill grandly entered, surveying the occupants of the biggest room in the building that he had insisted be made available for this meeting. Everyone stood and Tom Kennedy closed the door as he left. Cahill laid on the charm with the two ambassadors, lapping up their overtures.

The three sat at one end of the oval table, their officials watching silently from the other: the groups separated by the empty chairs. The envoys repeated to Cahill what they had been telling Mulligan, reminding the senator of Ireland's high standing in the developing world.

'My Commonwealth colleagues are still singing Ireland's praises for your leadership in concluding the signing of the Lomé Convention during your EEC presidency.'

The American made his contribution to the double charm offensive.

'President Carter has asked me to personally convey to you that he truly believes Ireland has a unique role to play in laying the groundwork for Rhodesia's future relationship with the West.'

'Such faith you have in us, Mr Ambassador. And, do please, give my best regards to Jimmy.' Pausing just long enough for the effect of his familiarity to sink in, Cahill gave a little laugh.

'Of course we all know the Soviet Union's low profile is a sham, that they are actively wooing the young African nations, that their denials of an alleged communist threat in Southern Africa are just part of Cold War double-speak,' Cahill told the American, both smiling in unison, underlining their shared understanding of the situation.

The excitable ambassador was fuelled by Cahill's sympathy. 'As you know, Senator, the Rooskies' denials are bullshit, if you'll excuse my French. Every left-wing guerrilla outfit in Africa seems to be armed with Kalashnikov assault rifles, churned out in the Soviet Union and Czechoslovakia. It's interesting that the Soviets seem to be doing a lot of arms dumping with the so-called "freedom fighters" in Rhodesia. They've been giving them the old Simonovs as well. Providing this bloody armoury was only one step short of putting troops on the ground themselves,' he added with a dismissive wave of his hand towards an imagined protagonist. He leaned forward as far as his large stomach would allow, pressing against the table, anxious to bring Cahill into his confidence.

'Between you and me, Senator, in 1977, just three years ago, we were lucky to expose a Cuban intelligence operation, no doubt inspired by the Soviets, designed to infiltrate agents into Rhodesia masquerading as Canadian mercenaries, supposedly willing to fight for the Rhodesian army. One of our own vets had signed up for it but blew the whistle when he saw through their little plan.'

Cahill frowned, acknowledging the trust the American was placing in him by providing such classified information.

'The Soviets are just part of the problem. We know that a lot of these guerrilla guys have been on the Peking payroll as well. Why, some of them have even been to China on training programmes,' the American added in exasperation.

'Of course, Rhodesia's strategic importance is not just as a potential supplier of valuable raw materials to the West, but as a linchpin in the future of Southern African politics,' Cahill added sympathetically in response to the American's frustration. The ambassador almost jumped in agreement.

'You betcha, Senator. You wait and see. Rhodesia goes commie today, South Africa tomorrow. Soviet subs and warships chugging around the Cape, all mining enterprises nationalised, threatening future supplies and exorbitant prices. Why, Senator, the prospect is...is... unthinkable.' The ambassador whined and took a pristine white handkerchief, the size of a pillowcase, from his pocket and mopped his forehead, exhausted at his diplomatic onslaught on the communists.

The British envoy spoke. Evenly. 'If the Soviets control the Cape route, in the event of war the West's enemies will be able to cut the world in two. It is essential,' he gave a hint of a bow towards his American counterpart, aware that he had grounds to be over-heated, 'it is essential, as we search for an equitable solution to the racial difficulties of Southern Africa, that we do not forget that fact.' He stopped for effect, and added, wanting to leave them with a profound thought, 'Communism is using the so-called "liberation" of Africa as a stepping stone in its own ambitions for world domination.'

The American ambassador's head bobbed in agreement. Cahill raised his eyes from the doodling he had started when the British envoy intervened. 'And you mean to tell me that it's my job to convince these guerrillas to row in with the West?'

Mulligan was expecting him to add, 'Now that's a tall order.' But Cahill just straightened his chin in a purposeful air. Mulligan was grudgingly impressed with Cahill's grasp of the situation. He had obviously read his briefing notes. And more.

Assessing the ambassadors' successful wooing of his very responsive senator, Mulligan could not understand why they had been so anxious to speak directly with him before meeting Cahill. As if anticipating his question, the American official opposite slipped a folded sheet of paper across the table. Ensuring the envoys had Cahill's attention, Mulligan peeped at the note: 'Springboks 15, Irish Anti-Apartheid Movement 6,000.' He knew exactly what the American meant. In January, 1970, the South African rugby touring side had met with fierce opposition to their match against Ireland at Lansdowne Road from 6,000 anti-apartheid demonstrators. A leading politician had made another indelible mark on the national consciousness when, megaphone in hand, he had led a counter-demonstration to the anti-apartheid protests, defending the Irish Rugby Football Union's decision, and made his way onto the front pages of the national papers in the process. It was an episode Senator Gerry Cahill no longer put on his CV. Mulligan now appreciated his role: to keep Cahill's racism in check.

Another sheet of paper appeared in front of Mulligan, this time from the British official, with just one word written on it. 'Moriarty?'

The question referred to a Patrick Moriarty, brought to Mulligan's notice the previous week by the British official, describing him as 'one of you Irish chaps who went native', and now seen as a conduit to Minister Julius Charamba, identified by British Intelligence as 'having Mugabe's ear'. After languishing in a dead-end job, being passed over for promotion year in, year out, Patrick Moriarty was reportedly enjoying his day in the sun since Julius Charamba became minister. Mulligan wrote the word 'zilch' in reply. There was no point in boring his opposite number with the details of the unreturned phone calls and unanswered telex messages.

The British ambassador was about to leave, his job done, pleased with the influence they had exerted on Cahill. The American also pushed back his chair and was levering his corpulence against the lacquered mahogany table to get on his feet.

'Tell me, Mr Ambassador, are you going to make any special arrangements to secure the repatriation of the pensions of British citizens who wish to leave Rhodesia?' Cahill, still seated, poised his pencil over the sheet of paper covered in drawings of boxes. The British envoy froze. His official threw a quick glance at Mulligan, asking silently, 'Where's this coming from?'

'Senator. Rhodesia is, Zimbabwe will be, a sovereign state, well-equipped to cater for its own public servants.' The British ambassador shifted, satisfied with his answer, feeling the advantage return to him. He moved his hands towards the back of the chair, reluctant to re-occupy it in case this discussion went too far.

'Does your government seriously expect the new regime to honour agreements with the servants of the old?' Cahill was upping the ante, asking the British representative for his government's view, rather than his own.

'Frankly, Senator, we must respect the new regime's ability to maintain the well-managed state that they are inheriting. We will be disposed to giving them all the assistance they need to maintain stability into the future. I'm afraid we cannot take responsibility for civil servants who choose…'

'Choose?' Cahill placed the pencil sharply on the table, emphasising his interruption. 'But didn't your government encourage these civil servants to stay in their posts. Why not take full responsibility? It is, was, a British colony after all. As one of your own said so eloquently, no new law ever saw the light of day in Rhodesia unless it had been agreed by your government.'

Watching the American ambassador slide back into his chair during these exchanges, his shoulders slumping, Mulligan thought for a moment that the deflated envoy would have slipped under the table altogether if his fatness had not wedged him in.

The British ambassador also sat down, finally acknowledging his breach of protocol. The American official at their end of the table winked at Mulligan, appreciating the discomfiture of the British. Mulligan allowed his lips to curl into an inkling of a smile. He knew Cahill was enjoying himself, but he could also hear the hard edge in his voice and wondered again about Cahill's real agenda. The livelihoods of former colonial civil servants would not have had a high priority normally with the senator. The British envoy placed his outspread palms on the table and inspected his manicured nails. He spoke directly to Cahill, weighing every word so that the Irish senator would have no doubt just how seriously he was treating his concerns.

'I believe, Senator, that your perceptive observations underline, if such were necessary, the very importance of your visit.'

Cahill appeared to hang on his every word, encouraging the British ambassador to share his wisdom. Mulligan had seen this too often before with Cahill, leading people in for a sucker punch.

'If, Senator, you can point Mr Mugabe and company towards the West, then I believe you will have made what possibly might be the major contribution in securing the future of the white administration and white Rhodesian population generally.'

The room was silent. Cahill continued to study the British representative, letting him know that he was expecting more of an explanation, until the Englishman broke away.

'Isn't that right, Mr Ambassador?' The British envoy directed his question at his American counterpart, who glanced towards his official at the end of the table for guidance. The crew cut, younger man shrugged, but the ambassador's heavy shoulders were not designed for a slight shrug and his attempt to repeat the gesture became a jelly of moving flesh. Cahill narrowed his eyes, a cobra about to strike. Mulligan cleared his throat, warning the senator that whatever about bear-baiting the Brits, annoying the Yanks - generally supportive of the Irish government on the Northern Ireland issue - was going to get them nowhere. Cahill re-fixed his vexation on the British representative.

'May I ask, Mr Ambassador, what will I tell the members of the National Farmers' Union? Who, by the way, have already asked to meet with me.'

The English official opposite Mulligan elaborately drew an imaginary question mark on the table. Mulligan jerked his head towards Cahill and winked, underlining this was nothing to do with him.

The British ambassador went pale, but all he said was, 'Senator?', letting his monosyllabic answer emphasise how strongly he disapproved of this line of questioning.

'I mean...like...'

Oh no, Mulligan wanted to shout, don't overplay your, 'I'm just a simple Paddy' game, as he listened to Cahill's feigned hesitancy.

'...what am I going to tell the white farmers about their land?'

The British envoy stared at Cahill but did not speak. There was no point. Cahill had him in a stranglehold. Why prolong the agony? Cahill waited, his cold eyes riveted on the silenced ambassador. Suddenly, he pushed back his chair and rose quickly, the British ambassador also getting to his feet immediately. Cahill waited until the American had prised himself out of his chair, and directed his question at the two officials at the other end of the table, leaving the ambassadors in no doubt that they had nothing more to offer.

'Well, gentlemen what will I tell them?'

In unison, the officials lowered their eyes, not wanting to be pounced on by Cahill.

'Will I tell them that their farms are secure? That the price for handouts from the West, for your, for our, support, will be for Messers Mugabe and Nkomo to stick to their side of the bargain and leave the white Rhodesian farmers continue to own, what you all appear to accept, is rightfully theirs?'

The English official jutted his chin forward when he spoke. 'I believe you know, Senator, that it is impossible to answer that question.'

Cahill scowled, accepting that the diplomatic double-speak was at an end. The official spoke towards his ambassador, who watched him impassively, giving no hint as to how far he should go. 'We cannot give any real guarantees. There simply aren't any. Despite what is written in the Lancaster House agreement, we cannot give the Farmers' Union, and the white farmers they represent, any real guarantees.' When he finished, he smiled weakly at Cahill. Mulligan wondered if the Englishman had some additional insight into Cahill's motives.

'Frankly, Senator, we fear for their future. Indeed, for the future of the whole white population.'

The words remained suspended in the high-ceilinged room. A phone could be heard ringing in the outer office. Acknowledging that he had probably said too much, the British official added, 'These are our concerns. Privately.'

Cahill moved towards the door.

'But Senator...'

'George?' Cahill used the British official's first name in appreciation of his frankness.

'Senator, I'm sure you now fully appreciate what the ambassadors said about the importance of your visit. Any hope we might have of securing the future of white Rhodesians is inextricably linked with our ability to establish...to repair...diplomatic...or shall we just say "relations" with Robert Mugabe. And, as you will be aware, it's not just about diplomacy and politics. We stood by while Ian Smith locked up Mr Mugabe for more than a decade, wouldn't even allow him attend his child's funeral, so Mugabe owes us nothing.'

'Thank you for your candour.' Cahill spoke directly to the British official, emphasising the word 'your'. After a calculated pause, he added, 'Good day, gentlemen' and left the room. Mulligan shook hands quickly with the two officials. He had a sneaking suspicion that they knew much more than he did, that they had seen the cards Cahill was keeping to his chest.

The telex message shakes in Minister Julius Charamba's hand, a name he thought he had deleted from his memory searing his brain. His overflowing emotions force him to his feet. He watches the early light coax the city of Salisbury awake. It is his favourite time of day, the sky is full of promise of fresh beginnings. The dream he has worked for all his life is now on the point of becoming a reality of new power and ownership, of new rights and privileges, banishing forever poverty, greed and inequality. This political dawn is for him an opportunity to prove the invaluable role he can play in the new government, not just to survive, but to thrive, like this emerging nation. Goodbye Cecil Rhodes and Rhodesia, hello to Zimbabwe,

Great Zimbabwe!

The sleeping city is slowly coming to life. Sounds of traffic drift up to his open fourth-storey window. His offices are overshadowed, literally and, most certainly he feels, metaphorically by the neighbouring thirteen-storey building, home to the more senior government ministries, casting a slab of grey across the rooftops of the Salisbury street below him. The sight of the shadows annoys him, reminding him that there is another height to climb in his ambitions for higher office. He lifts his face towards the distant, dull countryside, waiting to be coloured in by the rising sun, giving no hint of the turmoil it has endured, of the horrors it has witnessed in the years of fighting. Horrors he himself can only imagine, if imagine he dares. The mist is being burnt away quickly, revealing the endless horizon of the plain blending into the clouds so that it is impossible to distinguish between land and sky.

He waits for his trademark composure to return, and when he feels ready he counts to ten, wanting to ensure that no trace of the storm of memory remains. He lifts the phone from its cradle and dials three numbers, intently following each part-rotation. After just one ring, a voice gives the standard, curt, surname only reply. He hesitates, an actor about to enter from the wings,

'Ah! Mr. Moriarty, my dear chap, would you be kind enough to come to my office.' It is his most jocose tone, one he uses in private with the only white man in the building he trusts, who he tests by playing a joke with his name, asking, 'If I am Sherlock Holmes, who are you -Watson or Moriarty?'

The soft-spoken Irishman always gives the same answer. 'Minister, I am Moriarty by name only.'

He has played the little game many times, testing if the white civil servant will change his answer, do more than deny that he might be his nemesis and pledge his loyalty. But the answer is always the same, and he grudgingly admires Patrick Moriarty for that. After all, this is a time for keeping one's options open.

'What do you make of that, Patrick?' He uses the civil servant's full first name, acknowledging that this is how the Irishman consistently introduces himself, even though others abbreviate it to 'Pat' or 'Paddy'. As Moriarty cautiously studies the printout of the telex, addressed to him, playing for time, the minister asks in exasperation, 'What are they at? Does Senator Gerry Cahill not realise we have won the war. The old regime are already packing their bags. There is no one here worth talking to...'

The Irishman looks up in surprise. In that instant the minister understands what the civil servant was reading into the telex message, and reverts to his Sherlock Holmes persona.

'But then, my dear chap, perhaps Senator Cahill knows there is no one worth talking to except...' Charamba puffs on an imaginary pipe.

The Irishman's smile acknowledges the charade.

'Except...' The minister draws the imaginary pipe away from him, his chin rising as it follows his outstretched arm, a thespian fully into his role.

'Except me!' At that Minister Julius Charamba laughs, a melodramatic ha ha ha, making no effort to hide his bitterness.

Tom Kennedy carefully tied the laces of his runners, flexing his toes to prevent them getting too tight. He had a headache from the tension after yet another outburst from Cahill and the smoke around the table at the last meeting. If he detoured to Donnybrook he could trace the river Dodder nearly all the way to his housing estate in south Dublin, running through parkland most of the way along a path against the constant hurry of the river. He rotated his arms, limbering up, getting a buzz from the feeling of physical well-being.

Crossing over the canal at Leeson Street Bridge, he passed John Mulligan, smoking a cigarette, examining the stagnant water, shoulders hunched forward. The brooding Mulligan, witness to today's humiliation, only reminded him of the encounter with Cahill, and Kennedy quickened his pace, driven by the residual anger replacing his shame. He had been warned. The private secretary to Cahill in his last ministerial post had walked out of the Service. Just did not turn up for work one Monday morning and was never seen again. The rumour machine claimed he had run home to the small family farm in Kerry, and all letters had been returned unopened.

Kennedy despised Cahill. It was the only way he could deal with him. He despised everything about him, the good things and the bad: Cahill's reputation as one of the best politicians to absorb a brief; his superficial charm, switched on usually with great effect on both men and women, hiding from all - except those who had to work with him - the little bully boy always lurking just below the surface. He was learning quickly how to handle his temporary boss. When Cahill was in a good mood, he stayed aloof, keeping his guard up, watchful for the next flare-up. It was the only way to cope. As long as he did his job, he was safe from any major recrimination. The Secretary of the Department himself had promised early promotion when he inveigled Kennedy to take the assignment no one wanted. All he had to do was put up with Cahill for five days in Rhodesia. It would all be worthwhile, he told himself.

The sun caught the cascading whiteness where the Dodder loudly tumbled over a series of weirs. As he passed each little waterfall, easing the water's descent from the Dublin Mountains to the River Liffey at Ringsend, there was no sound to be heard other than the river living up to its Irish name: turbulent.

The run was erasing the memory of Cahill and the office. This was the stretch he liked most. Breathing at a steady pace, he exerted against the gentle uphill pull, feeling the sweat seeping through his pores, gathering at the small of his back. The previous night's celebration with his wife floated to the surface of his consciousness and swirled about. An ongoing debate between them on the timing of their next child, a brother or sister for Ronan, had been brushed aside on the strength of the Secretary's promise of a hike up the ladder, opening the way to a move to a bigger house. Sex. No, not sex. He mantra'ed The Golden Rule. Never think about sex while running.

He redirected his mind to the forthcoming trip to Salisbury. They would be among the city's first official visitors from an EEC country since the end of the Rhodesian war and the inauguration of the new Mugabe-led parliament. According to Mulligan, in any other circumstances the Brits should have been doing the bridge-building with the new leadership, but years of prevarication from Westminster after Ian Smith's Unilateral Declaration of Independence, and the deal they had brokered between the blacks and whites in the Lancaster House treaty, had not helped matters. Mulligan had laughed cynically when telling Kennedy this, saying the 'status quo go deo, more of the same forever' was what some of the white Rhodesians wanted. 'This so-called treaty was all about getting the Brits off the hook, an exit door from the last remnants of their colonial Africa. Ask yourself, Tom, if you had spent the last twenty years in the bush fighting over the ownership of the land, what would you settle for?'

His first trip to Africa: the idea made him nervous: not that he would admit it to anyone. At least Mulligan would know his way around, he told himself. Despite the Zambian debacle derailing his career, Mulligan was known as a shrewd operator. Kennedy laughed to himself at the craziness of an idea flitting into his mind: could he use the intimacy created by travel to ask Mulligan to verify the rumour that there were two African beauties in his room when his wife walked in?

On his recall to Dublin, and his public reprimand by then minister Gerry Cahill, Mulligan had been given the Southern African desk, token responsibility for monitoring a part of the world that mattered little to the Department of Foreign Affairs. With the IRA taking hostages in London, the SAS applying their own particular brand of terrorism on the ground in Northern Ireland, and so called 'tit-for-tat' killings a weekly event across the religious divide, the Irish government had enough on its plate from the 'Troubles' to stretch the Department to its limits as it launched charm offensive after charm offensive in Washington, Paris, Brussels and wherever else there might be a friendly ear.

21

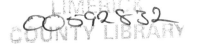

Mulligan had been given the kiss of death: a 'watching brief'. It was a classic Civil Service punishment for a man they could not easily sack: give him a non-job and hope he would leave or drink himself to death. Mulligan had almost obliged on the latter score and spent the first years on returning to Dublin boozing with a vengeance. Tom Kennedy did not know Mulligan at that stage, having only just joined Foreign Affairs, fresh from his honours degree in Literature at UCD. The grapevine whispers told the rookie Kennedy that this strange character with the Rasputin beard would not last long. John of God's alcohol clinic, cirrhosis, simple madness, were attaching themselves to his reputation.

But without warning Mulligan had confounded them all and gone on the dry. Even his drinking cronies within the Department were surprised, and he shrugged off enquiries with jokes about the 'road to Damascus' when people tried to probe his motives. The intensity Mulligan had applied to his drinking was diverted to his job. Soon he was acknowledged as the resident expert not just on Southern Africa, but on the whole continent. Mulligan's maps, in which he coloured in the progress of the Cold War in Africa, achieved notoriety in the Department's canteen. Mulligan updated them regularly, using red for communism and blue for capitalism, gleefully pinning each latest edition on the notice board, the frequency of change marking the instability of the region.

In 1975, while the Department basked in the glory of Ireland holding the presidency of the EEC for the signing of the Lomé Convention - the treaty between North and South that was reputedly going to change how the Third and First World countries dealt with each other - the Secretary of the Department had personally removed Mulligan's map illustrating developments in Angola. Just two weeks after its independence from Portugal, Soviet 'military advisers' had been confirmed in the beleaguered country, torn apart by a civil war between left-and right-wing factions in which thousands of people had already died. The Secretary did not object to the quick revision with Angola coloured in red, but at the bottom of the page Mulligan had written, 'I think I'm going to run out of red ink.'

*

Gerry Cahill moved his fingers over the bare flesh of the inside of her thigh, his face turned away, absorbing the passing night-time streetscape. He moved his hand further up, forcing her skirt higher. She drew in her breath sharply when he touched her sex, wet already, his index finger moving deeper into her. She was deadly silent now, perfectly still, staring at the back of the driver's head. This was their little game. Leaving the restaurant he had whispered to her and, after her coquettish display of histrionic outrage, she had gone to the ladies and removed her tights and panties. Cahill watched her face as he moved his finger gently inside her, altering the rhythm, her expression changing minutely in turn. She was breathing through her nostrils, mouth tightly closed, her teeth biting into her lower lip. The first time he had done this she had been nervous of the driver's presence, but she admitted afterwards it had added to the excitement. She tightened her grip on his knee, and shuddered. The side of her nose dimpled. She eased her lips apart, her eyelids drooping to almost closing. Later, she would strip completely while he remained clothed, watching him watching her. Then she would stand in front of him, tantalising, 'Do anything you want with me.'

Cahill had not bothered to check if Seamus had tilted the driver's mirror, sure of his discretion. Seamus had been his driver through four ministerial terms, a rare breed of a non-drinking, non-smoking and, most important of all, non-talking garda. In return for his tactfulness, for the hours of patient waiting late into the night while he 'attended to business', Cahill unquestioningly signed off on Seamus's generous overtime and expenses. When he lost his ministerial office, Cahill enticed the faithful guard to take early retirement, clinching the deal by promising to get an even bigger Mercedes than the E200 supplied to ministers.

Cahill vainly considered himself in the full-length mirror as he swished the towel across his shoulders. Compact but perfectly formed, he liked to call himself. Almost fifty, and he had no sign of a gut or any excess fat. Oh, your philandering will be the death of me, he silently told his flaccid member in his ongoing private joke as he pulled on his briefs. The front door bell rang once.

'Don't run away with any of those African women,' she called from the top of the stairs.

'My wife used to say the same thing about you Dublin girls.'

She laughed and cupped her naked breasts, pointing them at him.

The small, blue envelope had slipped from the manila folder on the back seat of the car. Cahill picked it up carefully, examining again the English stamp and the postmark from Heathrow Airport. Every time he had read the letter over the past fortnight he felt the stamp and postmark, confirming that the sender had been too afraid to post it directly from Rhodesia, said even more about the urgency of the situation than the words inside. He took the single sheet of blue notepaper from the envelope and unfolded it, only half-reading as the message was already imprinted on his brain, his older sister's awkward handwriting a reminder of her lack of formal education.

He knew she must have been very desperate to write that note, smuggling it out of the country to be posted by some messenger on arrival at Heathrow. Of course, he had rung immediately, but it was obvious from her oblique answers that she did not want to discuss it, not over the phone anyway. For days he had been at a loss, unable to see the next move. It was an unusual situation for Gerry Cahill, always so much in control. And then he heard about the leaderless diplomatic mission to Rhodesia and urgently made a few phone calls. Maybe he would be able to do something after all!

Patricia Lynch walked towards the diving board. She could feel her skin goose-pimple in the cool morning air. A few of the other regulars were about, but she ignored them, as always, before her swim, intent on getting into the water, afraid that she might chicken out if she stopped to talk and someone said it was colder than the day before. Pausing to confirm there was no one below her, she stepped off the end of the diving board. A split second of total freedom before she broke the cold morning water, feet first, nose held, allowing herself sink into the deep, tingling sea. Down, down, the cold enveloping her. Rising from the dark, breaking the surface with a gasp, she swam quickly away from the rocks, kicking her legs rapidly to warm up, the upper part of her body in a near perfect crawl, her shoulders rolling. The numb sensation was leaving her ankles. She rolled on her back, gazing up at the grey blanket of cloud. Lifting her head out of the water, she watched an old man shuffle to the end of the still-quivering board, where he straightened, sagging shoulders being pulled back, pushing himself high onto his toes, and then made a perfect dive, slicing almost soundlessly into the sea.

She walked quickly back to the apartment building, her long, white robe not sufficient to deter the ogles from bored drivers in snail-speed traffic. Predictable beeps from the more leery only added to her irritation. The hot water streamed over her tilted face, sluicing the sea salt from her short hair. Now she was ready for another day, and for the first time that morning she previewed what lay ahead, making a mental list of the things that needed to be done before she headed off to Zimbabwe.

She still could not believe her luck: everything had fallen into place so easily. When she heard there was a mission from Ireland going to the newly back-in-favour Rhodesia, she had wasted no time in making some discreet enquiries. She knew John Mulligan was on the Rhodesian desk, but would the Department let him go back to Africa? It would hardly be a full-blown diplomatic mission at such an early stage, so maybe they would trust him? She decided to go direct to Mulligan, feeling she knew him long enough to put her cards, or some of them at least, on the table. The less he knew about her real motives, the less harm it would do. She was surprised to learn that former Minister Gerry Cahill, recently foisted on the Senate, was going. According to Mulligan, they needed a political figure to give the delegation some status and to act as an icebreaker, but there was not one government minister available.

'Not even a junior. You can gauge from their collective lack of enthusiasm how successful they think our efforts will be, but the

Brits and Yanks are insisting we do something. The American ambassador keeps saying we have "street cred", whatever that means,' Mulligan told her.

'The palaver we're getting is that being a non-colonial power will give us a special status and the Yanks say that, if we're really stuck, we can play our "ace in the hole", and conjure up the good name of Bishop Donal Lamont.' Mulligan did not add any explanation, treating her as a fellow professional, appreciating that she knew that the Irish Bishop Lamont had been the most outspoken defender of the African struggle, despite the various efforts of the Smith regime to contain him, including about a year in prison before his eventual expulsion from Rhodesia.

'Our only problem is, Lamont is pretty pissed off with the Irish government at the moment. He feels we let him down over the years, and he's not bending over backwards to open any doors for us. So we'll just have to trade off his good name. The Brits have dug up some Paddy - by name and by birth - called Moriarty who is supposed to be close to Charamba.'

'Oh I've read about him. The academic.'

'The very man. He's been traipsing around the world on UN scholarships during UDI.'

'And your new found Brit friends hope that Charamba will be pro-West.'

'Exactly. At least not as "anti" as the rest. But he's seen as not as "bloodied" as the other ministers who have been in the bush or in prison, so he has a lot to prove to Mugabe. Like the new Zimbabwe, he's walking a tightrope.'

When John Mulligan told her the team comprised just Cahill, plus an acting private secretary and himself, she tentatively raised the possibility of she joining them. She was sure the aid agencies would welcome a first-hand assessment of the situation, and would have no problem convincing the main donors to endorse her inclusion. Her status as a seasoned emergency aid co-ordinator would ensure their support, and Rhodesia was something of a closed book because of UDI. There was a long sigh from Mulligan as he digested the proposition. She was just about to reiterate her case, when he simply said, 'I think that's a great idea. We have very little to offer these freedom fighters, so the promise of a few handouts might grease the way for us.'

She was grateful that he could not see her grimace at his choice of words and hoped he did not hear her sigh of relief.

'One condition, though.'

Patricia waited. She hated this horse-trading, but knew she had to play along. It was far too important to her to get into Zimbabwe as soon as possible.

'Anything.' Oh shit, she told herself, don't sound so desperate.

'Any?' Mulligan emphatically split the word. 'Thing?'

For one moment she thought he was going to proposition her, the idea coming into her head before she even had a chance to realise how ridiculous it was.

'Yes!'

She could hear Mulligan's voice breaking up. 'You'll just have to sleep with Cahill for four nights.' Then he let go, roaring with laughter. She hung up while he was still chortling down the line, and permitted herself a small laugh: one up for Mulligan. But she felt a rush of gratitude towards him. He had delivered. No 'ifs' and 'buts'. Even if the Department had tried to freeze him out, he was not afraid to make a decision. She knew he would convince anyone who needed convincing that her participation in the mission made sense.

Tom Kennedy tried to settle himself, his cramped knees pressing up against the seat in front, not looking forward to spending another nine hours like this. Planes were not designed with tall people in mind, he told himself, feeling the only consolation was that he was on his own. Cahill had, of course, regally taken his seat in first class, wallowing in the deference of the British Airways' hostesses. The British Foreign Office must have warned them to be extra nice to the Irish senator. Patricia Lynch and John Mulligan had opted for smoking seats. Feeling like a schoolboy who has not done his homework properly, Kennedy opened the manila folder and scanned Mulligan's briefing notes.

Currency: Rhodesian dollar (value approx. 95 pence).

Capital: Salisbury: pop. Approx. 380,000.

Population: black Africans constitute about 95% of the approx. 10 million pop: the two main African tribes are Shona (about 70%) and Matabele (about 25%.): the controlling white population number about 3%; 'coloureds' make up the rest.

Politics: The elections had eighty seats available to blacks: Robert Mugabe's largely Shona ZANU-PF, 57: Joshua Nkomo's ZAPU, drawing its support from the Matabele homeland, 20 seats. Mugabe's landslide victory is regarded by many, not just the white population, as a nightmare scenario.

Kennedy scanned through the paragraphs, words attaching themselves to his memory: abundant mineral resources, UK main trading partner, 10,000 mercenaries, breadbasket of Africa, whites kept all the good land, California-like sun, servants, swimming pools, sundowners. Kennedy re-read the paragraphs on the Unilateral Declaration of Independence.

In 1965, the white minority refused to accept political democracy, which would lead to black majority rule, as a British prerequisite for independence for its last colony in Africa. Led by Ian Smith, they made a Unilateral Declaration of Independence (UDI). Smith told the white Rhodesians, 'we have struck a blow for the preservation of justice, civilisation and Christianity and in the spirit of this belief we have this day assumed our sovereign independence.'

Commonwealth leaders in black Africa called on the British to crush the white rebellion, but the Labour government did not have the stomach to fight their white Rhodesian cousins. The white minority were also very loyal to the Crown and Smith claims that before he was forced to declare UDI, the Queen told Prime Minister Harold Wilson not to sell the white man down the river.

Initially seen as a bit of a joke, no one could have imagined that fifteen years later we would be only now approaching some form of democracy. The UDI regime was recognised only by South Africa after the UN imposed sanctions, including a half-hearted sanction on the supply of petroleum. If this one embargo had been properly applied, it is likely that UDI would have collapsed long ago.

Kennedy was going to skip the next page, but Mulligan's handwritten note drew him in.

Senator, you can take your pick from a or b:

a) The view held in London is that, of all the revolutionary campaigns in Southern Africa, Rhodesia has seen the most widespread use of terrorism by guerrillas. (Our own Bishop Donal Lamont has repeatedly said that we must be careful about the propaganda against the guerrillas.)

b) The Rhodesian army solution is to hold whole villages responsible for the presence of guerrillas: many people are killed for 'curfew breaking' or 'failing to halt' or 'caught in crossfire'. (Senator, they have obviously learned a lot from the Brits about euphemisms!)

Kennedy skipped on, unsure of what Cahill would have made of Mulligan's editorial comments, all the information and analysis adding to his unease about this visit to such a foreign-sounding environment. He jumped into the page where he thought he might see something familiar.

Irish links: number of Irish expatriates in Rhodesia is estimated at 80,000. Although he greatly angered our Irish-Rhodesian cousins, the arrest and expulsion of Bishop Lamont in 1977 for refusing to report the presence of guerrillas in his district is probably one of the best feathers in our national cap with the forthcoming black regime. Of course, many of our ex-pats have done well, and our links into the former Smith regime are good and include...

A frazzled woman with a small child on her hip was at Kennedy's row. For an awful moment he thought she was going to move in beside him. Sleepless nights had left him in an unfriendly mood towards small children. She shuffled on, examining her boarding card before using it to scrape the blonde hair from her face. The plane was quickly filling up, people squeezing past each other in the blocked aisle as belongings were loaded into the overhead compartments. Nearly every passenger had armfuls of parcels and shopping bags. Two black men sat in beside him, not returning his little 'hello'. They both wore Mao Tse Tung style tops, the round necks left open at the collar. The one next to Kennedy flicked through a copy of The Economist. He opened a page more widely, revealing it to his companion. Kennedy could just read the headline. 'Farmers' Union Urges British Government to Secure Land Guarantees.' The other man said something and they both laughed before the magazine was closed sharply and stuck into the netting on the back of the seat, provoking more laughter.

What language were they speaking? Shona? Ndebele? Part of Kennedy would have loved to ask them, but there was a distinct coolness towards him that was difficult to overcome. He listened to the roar of the jet engines, anxiously checking for some give-away sound signalling his imagined imminent plummet from the sky. Lights on the runway flashed by, blurred by the speed and the rain on the window. He felt an ache of love towards his wife as his fear multiplied with the rising angle of the plane. What if she were pregnant again already with the sister for Ronan that she kept hoping for?

Wanting to distract himself from thoughts of mortality, he delved into the manila folder again, holding the right side up as a screen. At the back of the file was an envelope with the words 'For Your Eyes Only' printed in imitation of a large stamp. The flap was sealed and Mulligan had written across it, 'Tom, this might give you a laugh. JM.' Kennedy gave a start when he slipped the sheet of paper out, checking quickly if the African men beside him could see what he was reading. The nearer had re-opened his copy of The Economist and was engrossed. His companion's eyes were closed, head firmly level, fingers spread on the knees of his razor-creased trousers, appearing to be meditating rather than sleeping. Kennedy glanced once more at the photocopy of the photograph of Cahill, megaphone in hand, leading the demonstration supporting the South African rugby tour. Then he carefully tore the sheet of paper through each crease into confetti and poured the pieces into the ashtray on the inside armrest, hoping his embarrassment was not obvious.

*

They stood on the tarmac in the cool morning air. It was still dark. Despite the distinct whiff of engine fuel, Mulligan could make out the smell of the vegetation. He breathed in deeply. 'Well, Tom, do you get it?'

Kennedy was half-asleep or overawed. 'It's...it's... like the smell of over-ripe fruit,' he ventured, checking to make sure no one had heard him.

'That, Tom, is the smell of Africaaa! Soak it up while you can. In a few minutes you won't notice it any longer. The sound effects too,' Mulligan continued with a proprietorial sweep of his arm, referring to the crickets whose chirping filled the morning air, 'will just fade into the background.'

A crew of black baggage-handlers was unloading their suitcases directly onto the tarmac. Some passengers were already rooting through the piles of luggage. The two men and Patricia Lynch joined in the scramble. Cahill moved away, imperiously surveying the empty stretch of runway. Mulligan helped Kennedy carry Cahill's bags, and they lurched their way towards the entrance of the building. They were near the end of the line. People were unnaturally quiet, craning their necks to see up the queue, anxious to have this stage completed. They spoke to each other in whispers only, and there was none of the usual excited babble after long-haul travel. Mulligan reckoned it was not just the effect of the overnight flight that was subduing his fellow passengers. The blacks in particular appeared nervous, self-conscious. How many of these, he wondered, were returning to their homeland for the first time since the white regime's Unilateral Declaration of Independence? Was he imagining it, or did most of the whites have an air of disappointment? Were they coming home to defeat? Or had they already tried to leave and found that the reality of an escape from black rule was very different to what was promised in the Lancaster House treaty?

'Where the F is their diplomatic channel?' Cahill asked loudly, appearing to address the question to the other passengers rather than the Irish delegation.

'They probably had no great need of one since 1965,' Mulligan replied, referring to Rhodesia's diplomatic isolation during UDI. Patricia Lynch made only a half-hearted effort to stifle her laughter. Even young Kennedy allowed a laugh to covertly escape. Mulligan noticed that just in front of him a distinguished black man, with grey curly hair and a little grey goatee beard, chuckled.

Finally, they were inside the narrow, single-storey terminal building, sparsely furnished with timber seating, and they could see the reason for their delay. The two white immigration officers were scrutinising every black person's passport and visa, asking short questions interspersed by long, sullen silences as they digested the replies. The whites were being waved through with only a cursory check of their documentation. Both officers were overweight with paunches that stretched their white shirts over their khaki shorts. The one processing Mulligan's queue had a pencil-line moustache and appeared to be wearing Brylcreem, his hair sleeked onto his scalp.

The two lines were almost silent, the blacks watching the interrogations nervously, the whites examining their feet to avoid being drawn into the scenes being played out under the naked fluorescent lights of the arrivals hall.

The English-accented voices of the immigration officials punctuated the quietness, greeting all passengers with pointed assertions, 'Welcome to Rhodesia.' 'Welcome to Rhodesia.' The documentation of the distinguished man who had shared in Mulligan's joke was attracting particular scrutiny from the Brylcreemed official, carefully examining the papers yet ignoring their owner. Mulligan strained to hear what he was saying in reply to the official's terse questions, but he was speaking too softly and all Mulligan could make out was 'UN. United Nations.' The progress of the other queue, slow as it was, underlined the impasse that appeared to have been reached in Mulligan's line. When asked again what his business was in Rhodesia, the man answered in a louder, exasperated tone, 'I am here, I am in Zimbabwe, on UN business.' He was not inclined to volunteer more information. The immigration officer continued to study the papers in his hand. Both queues were hushed, everyone watching. The other official had speeded up his checking of documents, and Mulligan felt he was making amends for his colleague.

Cahill had just taken a step to change lines when he was almost knocked over by a young black soldier in combat fatigues who leapt past him and grabbed the documentation from the Brylcreemed official, too busy in the sham examination of the papers to see him coming. The immigration officer angrily lifted his face. Leaning over the desk, the soldier placed his free left hand on the white man's shoulder, squeezing tightly, pressing him back into his seat, holding the documentation aloft in his right hand, daring the official to try and take it. Two more soldiers, armed with self-loading assault rifles, had arrived at the desk. Mulligan could see the sergeant's stripes on the first arrival, now leaning very close to the white man and whispering to him, mouthing the words as to a child. The official was trying to be impassive, until a flare of embarrassment reddened him from the top of his white shirt to his retreating hairline. The other immigration officer busied himself, beckoning people who had stopped to watch the scene to come towards him so that he could give them his attention and ignore the plight of his colleague.

Mulligan knew that whatever point the sergeant was making was underlined when he released the white man and, without a word to the UN representative, picked up his suitcases and stepped aside, encouraging him to precede him past the immigration desk. The two soldiers tensely gripped their rifles, unsure of what they should be doing. There was a hush around the building.

A sharp crack echoed off the tiled floor and wooden ceiling. Everyone turned at once. At the rear entrance one of the baggage-handlers, holding his hands aloft in exaggerated movement clapped again, and again, shifting his weight from foot to foot in a slow-motion dance. Suddenly, every black person in the hall was clapping, some laughing excitedly, others demure and polite. A woman in an ankle-length, bright yellow, African dress, her head in a red turban, started singing. A point in the distance directly over the head of the immigration officer remained the focus of the soldiers' gaze, intent on demonstrating their army training and impartiality. The baggage-handler did not change the pace of his slow handclap, keeping his eyes locked on the face of the immigration official as he approached the desk. Mulligan realised what naked hatred looked like.

The singing woman raised her hands over her head so that her fingers arched together, swaying her hips in rhythm. Mulligan watched, unable to understand the words, until she came to what sounded like a chorus, taken up with gusto by most of the other Africans.

'Zim-zim-zim-babwe.' 'Zim-zim-zim-babwe.'

The two-door, light green Ford Anglia was in remarkably good shape, considering it was probably older than its young driver who silently took charge of them, somehow squeezing their baggage into the boot. Cahill commandeered the front passenger seat, the others cramming into the back with Kennedy crushed in the middle, his long legs almost touching his chin. The driver did not reply when Mulligan told him 'Meikles Hotel'. None of the garrulousness of taxi drivers here, Mulligan told himself. The taxi man's wordlessness imposed itself on the car as they drove towards Salisbury on a road better than anything in Ireland, except for the short stretch of dual carriageway heading south from Dublin. The edges, where the tarmac met the red-brown earth, were neat, everything evenly finished. Mulligan contemplated the small industrial units lining the roadside, all well maintained with little sign of one of the hallmarks of postcolonial Africa: peeling paint. When they reached the leafy outer suburbs of Salisbury, Cahill prised himself upwards in his seat and stretched his head back so far that Patricia Lynch, sitting behind him, could see the upturned whites of his eyes. He spoke to the roof of the car.

'When discussing "aid" Mizzz Lynch, you might ask if they can sort out our roads as well.'

It was the first time Mulligan had heard the recently imported, American- manufactured, address 'Ms.' being spoken. It was clear that Cahill saw the term as reserved for what he perceived as lesbians and women's libbers. Any possible humour in his comment was lost through his open dislike of Patricia Lynch. From the moment she and Gerry Cahill had met, at a briefing by the aid agencies when Cahill was minister, the hostility between them had been undisguised. Cahill had been uncomfortable with this strident, yet very attractive, female who made it quite clear she was not susceptible to his charms.

The hotel porters loaded the luggage onto handcarts, watched mutely by the driver. Kennedy was left to settle the fare as Cahill lead the way into the hotel, both glass doors being opened by invisible hands as he approached. The foyer was dark after the brightness of the street. As his eyes adjusted, Mulligan considered the solid, dark furniture with white lace mantles sitting on the headrests of the crimson and blue upholstered chairs.

Kennedy was at his shoulder, jumpy with news. 'He'd no tongue,' he whispered dramatically to Mulligan.

'The taxi driver! I swear to God. The poor bastard had no tongue!'

'Ciúnas!' Mulligan's use of the Irish word, as a teacher hushes a child, stung him. Kennedy, unsure now, apprehensively checked to see who had heard "his news from the war front" as Mulligan later jokingly called it.

As far as Mulligan could see, all the patrons were white and all the hotel workers were black, except for the receptionist, a woman in her mid-thirties who was uncannily like Jackie Kennedy. She greeted them now with a polite, 'Good morning, gentlemen.' The toothy, standard American welcomes had not yet caught on in Rhodesia. Yes, everything was arranged, they had received their telex booking. Sorry, they did not have a super-executive suite for Senator Cahill, but they had reserved the rooftop penthouse. She hoped this would be all right. Cahill was delighted, his status getting due recognition. Tom Kennedy filled out the forms for Cahill and himself. They were given rooms on separate floors.

'Are we in ascending order?' Mulligan said just loud enough for everyone to hear, wanting to deflate Cahill. Patricia laughed. Kennedy increased his concentration on the form filling, bending over even more to prove that he was not hearing any jokes. Cahill remained impassive.

'At least we won't be falling over each other,' Mulligan added in response to the receptionist's anxiety. Smiling for the first time, she invited them to 'partake of breakfast while housekeeping finished their rooms'.

Mulligan's bedroom was furnished in a similar heavy style to the foyer. The headboards and footboards were made of some dark wood with intricate carvings of elephant heads on the corner posts. A writing cabinet that appeared like a genuine antique, with a matching four-legged stool, together with two low armchairs covered in chintz material, made up the rest of the furniture. Everything was spotlessly clean. The corner of the bedspread had been folded back to reveal starched white sheets and on the pillow was a small chocolate bar, with the words 'Meikles Hotel' printed in gold on the purple wrapper.

From his eight-floor vantage point he could see across the city centre into what appeared to be suburbia. It was hard to imagine, cocooned by all this order and old-world grace, that a famine was threatened just a few miles away. The heat was very dry. Salisbury, the 'sunshine city', benefited from its high altitude and did not suffer the humidity that was the plague of most of Africa. 'California-like', one of the guidebooks from the early sixties had called the exceptionally high standard of living and abundant sunshine.

'But what the guidebook does not tell you,' Mulligan had earlier cautioned Kennedy, 'is that "exceptionally high standard of living" was enjoyed by the three percent white population who controlled the country, who had created a lifestyle where nearly every white man, even lowly civil servants like us, not to mention tradesmen such as electricians and plumbers, could afford a house with a swimming pool and at least one servant.'

In a poor attempt at a posh English accent, Mulligan had continued, 'Of course, the less well off might share a gardener with their neighbours, but that was no great hardship as their smaller suburban gardens do not merit full-time care and, as we all know, it's best to keep the black servants busy: otherwise they only get up to mischief.'

Mulligan smiled to himself as he recalled Cahill's stone-faced observance of his playful lecture to Kennedy and wondered again why did he seem so annoyed at Mulligan for lampooning the White ruling class.

Thirsty after the rashers served as part of the 'traditional English breakfast', Mulligan was mildly surprised, considering how meticulous the service had been since they arrived, to find that the cold-water flask beside his bed was empty.

'Of course, sir, we will send a boy immediately,' Room Service told him, answering his call after just one ring. He returned to his window-gazing.

Africa. He never thought he would see this place again. Africaaa!

A passion for Irish music had brought them together, squashed against each other in O'Donoghue's, where the whole city appeared to have crammed into the small, dark bar to hear one of the new groups reinventing traditional music. On escaping to the job in Dublin, Mulligan had quickly adopted the uniform of almost every other man in the pub: he had grown a beard, a passport to this world, where Fidel Castro was celebrated for freeing Cuba, and pints were raised to the health of Nikita Khrushchev and the Dalai Lama. There could be no mistaking him for an off-duty soldier or guard. It was this very beard that brushed against her forehead as she tried to retrieve her drink from the bar. He stretched out over her head and the scrum of bodies and lifted the pint of Guinness, presenting it in mock ceremony, marking the contrast in their height that would pick them out from the other couples swarming onto Grafton Street on Saturday afternoons.

'It beats pursuing the hapless taxpayers,' he almost shouted into her ear, gesturing towards the swell of bodies and the demonic musicians in the corner. He was taking a chance, deliberately letting her know he had seen her before and had made some enquiries about her.

'And what makes you think I'm in "The Revenue",' her arch tone telling him that she was flattered by his advances. 'Do I seem like a stuffy old civil servant?'

'Even if you were old, I cannot imagine you ever being "stuffy".' He was pleased with his attempt at gallantry. So was she.

Their wedding was planned as a low-key affair, opting for the University Church on St. Stephen's Green rather than return to her home town of Waterford. 'I don't want them all coming to gawk at me,' Kate said with venom.

Her father refused to have anything to do with it, her mother travelling without him, making a unique stand in her own rigid marriage. John Mulligan's parents fussed over Kate and her mother in an apologetic way, wanting to make recompense for their son's transgressions. The young couple floated above the guilt that many felt they should be carrying. Kate refused to wear white. 'I'm not the fucking Virgin Mary, you know,' she told Mulligan as she sipped her glass of Guinness in the snug in McDaid's. Their priest, a returned missionary friend of Mulligan's, chose the reading of 'let him without sin cast the first stone', leaving the congregation in no doubt he did not want any hypocritical condemnation of Kate's pregnancy. Mulligan's colleagues in the Department of Foreign Affairs thought it was all very bohemian, reflecting their more liberal views imported from foreign travel.

The evening wedding reception underlined their non-conformity. Mulligan listened to his best man's too-long introduction, anxious to get to his feet, when one of the strays came in from the bar, stone-faced, whispering something to the people nearest to him as he sat down. They gasped and Mulligan watched the news leap from person to person, some instinctively making the sign of the cross. Women started to cry. The best man concentrated on his laboured, scripted speech, droning on across the drama flowing through the room. The news was reaching the top table. Father Michael leaned towards Mulligan's dad, shaking his head in disbelief. Mulligan could hear 'has been assassinated, has been assassinated', people holding this foreign word on their lips, full of political upheaval, reserved for the killing of statesmen. When his moods were blacker, as they increasingly became, Mulligan would see in JFK's assassination some kind of omen, foreboding the decline of his own marriage.

They used the gratuity paid to Kate when she left the Civil Service because of the 'marriage bar' to furnish the flat they had rented on Waterloo Road, wanting to stay in the city, resisting the pressure to move to one of the new suburbs out beyond Rathgar, "out in the sticks" as the native-Dublin porter in the Department called it. Kate sent a frisson through the imagined Bohemia of 'Jule's' when she insisted on breastfeeding Claire in the restaurant. The bouncing baby became a sort of mascot in the pubs they called into in the early evenings and Sunday mornings. They regularly arrived back to the flat to find the place filled with smoke from the cremating roast in the oven, the potatoes hard as rocks, and laughingly sliced deep into the meat through the burnt crusts to salvage enough for sandwiches, washed down by bottles of Guinness and Matheus Rosé. Claire was thriving through it all, falling asleep in the noisy bars, her head on Mulligan's chest, blonde curls interweaving with his beard's blackness. She took her baby steps through the narrow passageway of the Waterloo Bar on a Sunday morning to the admiration and applause of the assembled drinkers, the few women present particularly taken by the golden-curled princess.

Kate said that if he were a boy they should call him 'Nelson', as it was surely the night they celebrated the blowing up of Nelson's

39

Pillar that their second child was conceived. This pregnancy was much more difficult. Morning sickness seemed to last all day. She lost all interest in going to the pub, reminded Mulligan that Claire was getting too big anyway, but did not seem to mind when Mulligan retained the same patterns of drinking after work. Often he would forget the time and sneak up the creaking stairs, fumbling with the key in the lock, glad to find them both asleep, Claire at right angles to her mother in the same bed. Mulligan opting for the couch rather than disturb them, sleep coming fast, despite the cramped conditions.

His earlier elation at getting the Barbie dolls for the girls, the Christmas shopping complete, gave way to gloom as he told the lads in the Waterloo Bar about the pressure he was under to move to suburbia. Holding back, despite the drink, from also talking about the alienation he felt, watching his best friend and one-time drinking companion settle into motherhood and domesticity.

A lifeline came out of the blue, on the New Year's Eve after that near-disastrous Christmas. Mulligan's gut-wrenching fear on getting the summons to the Secretary's office was quickly washed away by the unusual warmth of the welcome. The Secretary gave a tortuous preamble about the government's commitment to the newly developing countries, that they must refocus their efforts away from just the established diplomatic links, about how important this venture would be for the Department. Mulligan feared what kind of a pup he was being sold, particularly as he listened to the Secretary explain that, when they considered who would be the best man for this important, ground-breaking assignment, they wanted someone with stability in his life.

'No point in sending off one of our gay, as in carefree, you understand, Mr Mulligan, bachelors who might be led astray too easily,' he said dryly.

It was the most humorous remark Mulligan had ever heard him make. Then the Secretary revealed his grand plan. As part of its new commitment to fostering relations with the emerging states in Africa, the Department was opening an office in the Zambian capital,

Lusaka. It would not have full embassy status, yet, but it was the ideal environment for an able first secretary to make his mark.

Zambia!

Africa!

The timing was perfect. Mortgages and house-hunting were all swept aside. They could use the money they would save on rent to put together a deposit on a house. Most important of all, Mulligan privately saw it as a chance to break away from the drinking habits that seemed to be swallowing up his life.

Lusaka was seen as a hardship post, so no expense had been spared in creating comfortable living quarters. The Department had acquired a self-contained compound that had been built by an Englishman who had gone home suddenly after Zambia got its independence. Behind the timber walls, topped off by barbed wire, was a six-bedroom house with separate servants' quarters. The swimming pool was small, but deep and refreshingly cool. A neat hedgerow cordoned off the private quarters from the remainder of the buildings, comprising a suite of rooms that were fitted out as offices. Mulligan flew the tricolour from dawn to dusk and had flags painted on the walls of the compound, beside the words 'Éire-Ireland' in glaring white. No harm in letting people know there was a new owner. He threw all his energy into the new job and into bringing the house back to its one-time glory as a colonial haven in the suburbs of Lusaka. He wanted everything to be just right when Kate and the girls joined him in May, at the start of the cool season, giving them a chance to acclimatise in temperatures more akin to a good Irish summer. He was the only Irish official. Two clerks, hired through contacts with the local Catholic secondary school, made up the staff complement and they occupied themselves arranging the occasional visas for visiting businessmen and frequent requests from Zambian students to be allowed travel to Ireland.

Zambia was overflowing with excitement, bursting from celebrations of freedom. The streets of Lusaka were filled with people talking, laughing, men holding hands as they told each other stories, heads leaning to the sky in laughter, women busy with work

41

and childminding, gracefully balancing on their heads parcels that appeared too heavy to lift, sailing through the busy markets. He was enthralled, catching the infectiousness of what seemed to be permanent festivities. But the evenings were sometimes longer than he liked. Work finishing early, by four-thirty, made them seem even more drawn-out. He wrote to Kate every night, taking more than an hour or more to tell her every detail of the improvements he was making to the house, wanting to impress on her that he was mending his ways without ever having to admit it.

Weekends were proving difficult to fill. He was becoming known on the embassy circuit, ensuring that Friday nights were always spoken for. But the invitations were less frequent for Saturdays, reserved for smaller dinner parties, a wifeless Mulligan difficult to fit among the couples.

He went to mass on Sunday mornings. It was expected of the only official representative of the Irish government. Eleven o'clock mass, most favoured by the expatriate community, giving an hour to socialise before lunch. On his first morning the priest, a native of Cork city, welcomed him from the altar and jokingly encouraged him to come forward to the front pew on the right hand side. He discovered afterwards it had been deliberately left empty for him. The next Sunday, when he arrived just before eleven, the same pew awaited him. Overcoming his self-consciousness, he occupied it again, wishing Kate and the kids were there to hide his aloneness.

The African houseman was anxious that Mulligan would be late for mass. Afraid to call out his boss's name, the elderly man's knocking on the bedroom door increasing in tempo, dragging Mulligan out of a drink-induced stupor. Always a bad sign to be still wearing his pants, Mulligan told himself as the end of the night came back to him. Writing to Kate, he had been gripped by an acute loneliness, catching him unawares after a pleasant day in the compound, enjoying the sun after three days of rain, dividing his time between the pool and the James Bond novel discarded by the previous owner. He had nibbled at the cold meat supper, the words of his daily letter coming hesitantly this evening. Swirling the whiskey, well diluted with the melting ice, he examined the cloudless African sky, twinkling with a myriad of pinholes. Unable to write any more, restless under the moonless blackness, he leafed through the well-thumbed copy of A Soul for Sale, one of the few relics from what he now thought of as his "mad days" when all he wanted was a book of poetry and a pint of Guinness.

The feeling of loneliness, of insignificant nothingness, gripped him like a physical thing. It was all a sham, this poncing around the embassy circuit, Mercedes nudging Mercedes in the driveways, the polite charades being acted out by people who seemed to believe them. He in the thick of it, Mulligan the would-be poet, the sensitive soul, sold out. He knew this demon well. This demon eating up his self-belief. That made him want to smash his fist into the... into the... he never knew what. Just smash out in some anger of being angry. He swished the remainder of the tumbler of whiskey around his mouth, trying to wash away the dryness. When he awoke, the empty bottle lay on his lap. He thought he had been asleep all night, but it was only one in the morning. A long evening, he had started early, he told himself, staggering into the bedroom.

The smiling houseman was reassured to see him finally make an appearance, and fussed sympathetically around his sullenness, assuming something must be terribly wrong for Mr John to be so angry on this lovely Sunday morning. He allowed the day to take its course, wanting his mood to be washed away by the everyday patterns of breakfast, shower, the car pulling up to the house, his dark-suited driver standing patiently under the heat of the sun, the routine trip through the well-tended suburbs into the busier streets of the city, the church pew, his pew, waiting patiently like his driver, like his houseman, all patient with the whims of the white man.

After mass, Mulligan insisted on walking. His head was pounding, and he could not face the built-up heat of the car. The driver tried to shadow him, but Mulligan insisted he would make his own way back. The church nestled in a small, dusty square separated from the main street by a thronging marketplace. He picked his way through the chaotic aisles, stall blending into stall, sounds of chickens and goats competing with the babble of voices, everyone talking loudly and, all around him, laughter. A man held up a long, multicoloured dress, calling out to Mulligan, 'For the missus, for the missus.' Mulligan shook his head, the movement more pronounced by his wide-rimmed straw hat. He must have appeared very lonely in his sombre mood, and the dress salesman shook his head in turn in sympathy. A woman selling nearby loudly said something and her browsing customers all laughed, particularly the women. Mulligan smiled, a weak trace across his lips, the best he could muster in his hangover, demonstrating that he knew the joke was on him.

He was relieved to get on to the street with its wide footpaths and Paw-Paw trees providing intermittent shade. He had a terrible thirst on him.

Lusaka International Hotel had seen better days, the peeling paint eloquently telling of its decline, neglected during the closing years of colonialism. Mulligan passed the empty reception desk towards the unmistakable sounds from the bar. He stepped from the gloomy corridor into an after-match pub scene from home: animated revellers everywhere, chatting, laughing, smoking, drinking. People moving comfortably from cluster to cluster, like one big party.

There was an almost imperceptible twitch of uncertainty from those nearest to him when they became aware of the new arrival, the only white man in the room. It was easy to decide what beer to drink. There was only one on draught, lager-light in colour and taste, washing the taste of the whiskey from the back of his mouth. He was debating should he have another one, knowing he was breaking all the guidelines issued by the Department, when the barman presented him with a full pint and indicated that he should look behind him. Mulligan found himself facing a beaming, heavy-featured man, surrounded by the biggest crowd in the bar, his cream suit and cravat underlining his superior rank.

Mulligan was left in no doubt as to what he should do next. The group parted, making room for him to approach the centre of their attention, who squeezed his hand warmly, smiling a flash of white teeth contrasting with a gold crown on his left incisor. With an expanse of his free hand, he said, 'Welcome to Zambia.'

Tumani Mbebe (a claimant to be a distant cousin of the Zambian president, as Mulligan found out later), introduced Mulligan to the men in his circle, each shaking hands strongly with him in turn. Mulligan found out later how novel this was for them, to be with a white man on an equal footing. In answer to their openly curious questions, he told them a little about himself, emphasising the Irish Government's wish to build stronger links with the newly-liberated Zambia. He broached Ireland's identification with Zambia, a shared history of British occupation. Some of his audience laughed knowingly, and one of them lifted his pint, declaring, 'To James Connolly,' enjoying Mulligan's surprise at the mention of the socialist rebel. A tray of drinks was delivered. Mulligan was reassured to see he was not the only one who had finished his pint. He had not noticed anyone ordering, and the same pattern was repeated just when he was about to get another round.

The three girls beckoned Mbebe away from the centre of the group. He laughed a lot as they appeared to be cajoling him, each taking turns, one of them linking his arm and pressing herself close to his big stomach. Eventually, Mbebe threw his arms to heaven in pretend despair.

'You have a fan club, John.' He indicated the young women with a sweep of his hand, a shyness overtaking them now that they were face-to-face with Mulligan, who was at a loss, uneasy with the open sexual curiosity. He did not want to do anything that would ruffle the other men, but they were busy arguing over a soccer match, and he wordlessly appealed to Mbebe for guidance. The grinning Zambian lifted his drink and toasted Mulligan, 'Welcome to Lusaka.' Then Mbebe laughed heartily as the prettiest of the girls, emboldened by his encouragement, slipped her right arm partly around Mulligan's waist and with her free hand stroked the Irishman's long beard.

Returning to the Lusaka International Hotel the next Sunday, he found the scene in the bar was almost the same. Tumani Mbebe, surrounded by his collection of hangers-on and friends, waving him into their company, acceding to Mulligan's insistence that he be allowed buy a round of drinks. Any self-consciousness Mulligan felt about disappearing with the girl was soon forgotten when he realised that the others appeared not to have noticed. When Dorothy or Doreen (he was unsure of her name afterwards when he slipped out of the hotel bedroom, leaving her with more than enough to settle the bill) approached him, she seemed a little shy, holding back, wanting to get Mulligan to engage with the young woman who was with her, introduced as her sister with lots of giggles and flashing eyes.

Within a month Mulligan was calling to the Lusaka International Hotel on Wednesday evenings as well as on Sundays after mass, his driver waiting patiently for him, insisting it was too dangerous for Mr. Ambassador to be walking around the city after dark. By the time Kate and his daughters joined him he was hooked, the patterns well-established.

His daughters loved the drama of parading up the church, sliding impudently into the empty pew, Kate reluctantly following them, forewarned by Mulligan as to what was expected of her.

'Why, you must be Mrs Mulligan, Welcome to our humble, little church. And I hope you're settling in. I'm sure himself must be glad to have his family around him again. It can't be easy being on your own when you're not used to it.'

Travelling back to the compound, Mulligan guiltily surmised that the Cork priest was trying to give him some sort of hint. Staring out the car window at the dilapidated shells of unfinished buildings giving way to the opulent suburbia of embassy belt, Mulligan caught himself brooding, hiding his innermost thoughts behind a mask of preoccupation.

That first Sunday afternoon he directed his emotions at the children, trying to use their laughter to neutralise the smouldering cocktail of guilt and lust. Kate happily watched from behind the large sunglasses covering most of her face. Later, as she rubbed cream on his sunburnt shoulders, she moved her flat palm down his back into his shorts.

Wednesday was a sacrosanct stag poker night with a few of the lads. This was the excuse Kate trusted, content with the attentiveness she had received since her arrival the previous Friday. In an unspoken understanding that there was a new dimension to Mulligan's domestic life, when he arrived at the hotel on Wednesday night no one enquired about his absence on Sunday, and nobody ever asked why he did not come in after mass anymore.

Kate's biggest problem was getting the houseman to cooperate. He particularly resented her wanting to go to the market and addressed all his questions to Mulligan, took all his orders from him. Kate was amused, satisfied to go along with the situation, uncomfortable anyway with the idea of having servants to boss around. Encouraged by the other embassy wives, who empathised with her problem, she gradually asserted her position, but she never succeeded in generating the warmth exhibited towards Mulligan.

'What a life!'

Mulligan raised his glass in agreement, celebrating their first month in Zambia.

'No housework. Permanent babysitters. A woman could get very used to this provided she didn't run out of good books.'

The Mulligans were popular at parties where Kate would sing, her haunting voice escaping into the African night. Mulligan resisted all attempts to persuade him to reveal a party-piece, content to leave Kate as the centre of attention and also certain that the only songs he knew, the rebel songs a zealous schoolmaster had beaten into him, would probably not go down too well in these polite, diplomatic circles.

The significance of seeing his driver standing at the door of the bar of the Lusaka International Hotel did not register with him immediately. He had momentarily forgotten the sacking incident. Peculiar really, as it was the bile because of what happened between the driver and himself that had him drinking more quickly than usual that very evening, his fictitious 'poker night'. Encouraged by Kate, who could see how edgy he was when Mulligan had told her of the driver's dishonesty, he had taken a taxi to town. The game of cards with the lads would do him good, she told him sympathetically.

He was standing now with his hand on the backside of one of the 'lads', the young, tall, black woman resting her head into his shoulder. As it finally dawned on him that his former driver should not be there, Kate appeared next to the forlorn Zambian, witnessing the scene of unfaithfulness, everything falling into place for her.

'Don't say a word! He's given me chapter and verse. Every moment of his waiting on your whoremongering. Driving you, you…' Her voice trailed off.

The girl detached herself from Mulligan and moved a short distance away, afraid of the glaring white woman. Nudges and shushes were drawing attention to the showdown. But the gaping spectators were disappointed when the white woman left abruptly, leaving only an anti-climax behind. The driver slipped away in Kate's wake, her driver now, temporarily at least, until his revenge could be executed. All faces were directed towards Mulligan. The choice he had to make clearly spelt out to the watching drinkers. Mulligan reached out his arm and drew the girl back towards him while he drank with his head tilted back. He held the empty glass high, a clear signal to the barman. The barman took another from below the counter and pointed it towards him, his dumb show confirming that Mulligan really wanted more. Mulligan laughed in affirmation, squeezing the girl into him.

He spent the night in the hotel, the first time he had made full use of its often-rented rooms. Overcoming the temptation to just stay away until Kate had left with the children, knowing she would want some pretence maintained for their sake, he went home briefly and told them he must go away for a few days to visit one of the Irish government-funded projects upcountry. When he returned there was no trace of his family at the compound: no clothes, no dolls, no bathing costumes drying on the bars at the pool. He found out afterwards Kate did not stay in Dublin even for an afternoon, continuing her journey directly to Waterford, back to her father's house, confirming his predictions of his daughter's doomed marriage.

*

The single knock on the door snapped him from Zambia to Zimbabwe.

'Come in,' he called, facing out the window, reluctant to let go of his thoughts.

'Excuse me, massa.'

Mulligan turned and stepped back in surprise. The UN diplomat who had been escorted through the airport by the army sergeant was in front of him, holding a tray with a jug of iced water: same hair, same goatee beard, same distinguished face, but wearing a white uniform of short-sleeved shirt and short pants. It was also apparent that this man did not have the composure of his UN doppelganger. He was consternated by Mulligan's reaction, his widening eyes asking the question, had his opening of the door too quickly startled his hotel guest?

'I'm sorry.' The man bowed apologetically in the doorway. 'You rang for water. Massa.'

Mulligan brusquely indicated the empty flask, annoyed at himself for being so taken aback, not just at the likeness between the two men, but more so for forgetting the colonial language that had so often borne the brunt of his sarcasm. He had been expecting a 'boy' to appear, as promised by Room Service, not this man, older than himself.

I know letter writing is a bit silly. When I saw the airmail envelope in the room, I decided to drop you a quick note. I'll probably be home before it. We're here. Safe and sound. Dispersed to our rooms. Cahill is getting a real swelled head, a big fuss made to get him some kind of penthouse. Mulligan is in his element. Like a tour guide. He gave us a little lecture over breakfast on pronunciation of African names starting with two consonants. Just say the first consonant separately. Very simple really, he says, but I keep trying to bite off the two together. I think the lecture was for

49

Cahill's benefit.

Can't make an awful lot out of the Lynch woman. There's no love lost between herself and Cahill. She's very good-looking. But you needn't worry. I think she's a lesbo. She's a little bit old for me anyway.

Everything is very civilised here so far. The hotel is real olde worlde. Very posh, kind of like the Shelbourne.

We saw a really great scene at the airport. Tell you all about it when I get home. And remind me to tell you about the taxi driver. I get the feeling Cahill might be getting a chilly reception.

Give Ronan a big hug. And for yourself!

Tom Kennedy waited in his room just long enough to feel certain that Cahill in particular had settled down and then headed back out again, handing the airmail envelope to the receptionist on the way. He found it difficult to understand how the others could be so blasé about what was happening. Here they were, among the first official witnesses to Rhodesia-Zimbabwe's 'new dawn', and all they wanted was to rest after their journey. The excitement of being in Salisbury had him wide-awake. Too late, he remembered the sunglasses in his suitcase. He was stung by the brightness and stood momentarily outside the hotel, a prisoner of indecision.

The footpath was quiet, pedestrians mainly strolling, a few cars driving unhurriedly through the wide street. In some ways the scene resembled a sixties American film, or one of those old postcard photographs of O'Connell Street, with its out-of-date cars and clothes. He had read about the layout of the city in the guidebooks, but the simple 'Third Street' took him by surprise. It reminded him of his student days in New York, this naming of streets by numbers. He felt a sudden sense of anti-climax. It all seemed so 'un-African'. The streets and avenues intersecting, again underlining the newness of the city with its even rectangles, all parallels and perpendiculars, unlike the meandering streets of his native Galway, running into each other like streams. 'Stanley Avenue.' This was more like what he was searching for, a touch of history, European history overlaid on African, but history and not just numbers. He was trying to soak up what he was seeing, underscoring the experience by reminding himself, 'I am on the corner of Third Street and Stanley Avenue, in Salisbury, in Rhodesia, in Rhodesia-Zimbabwe about to become Zimbabwe, in the middle of Africa. If my ma could see me now.' If only his wife could be with him to share this experience. What would his three-year-old, Ronan, make of it all? Across the road he could see the sign for Cecil Square, surrounded by the famous Jacaranda trees shown in all the guidebooks with their purple September flowers.

All the surrounding buildings were low rise, none more than four storeys, dominated by what looked like a new wing of Meikle's Hotel.

'One of the few signs of the effects of the war on Salisbury is the lack of development as resources were diverted to more urgent matters.' He even remembered the way Mulligan had underlined 'more urgent matters' in the briefing note. He looked at the signs again, 'Third Street, Stanley Avenue', framed against the clear blue sky, and wished he had brought his camera.

'Can I help you?' An American voice abruptly ended his daydreaming. He swung around to see a black man, as tall as himself, smiling broadly. 'You seem as disorientated as I've been for the past two weeks.'

Kennedy shrugged, at a loss to explain himself, still off balance from his encounter with the taxi driver whose reaction to the over-generous tip had revealed the stump in his mouth. 'Is it that obvious I'm a newcomer?' He spoke hesitantly, shading his eyes against the sun.

'Way...ell, you're not brown enough to be a white Rhodesian,' the stranger said as he burst out laughing, adding, 'I had better remember that for my next dinner party.'

Kennedy was trying to hide his uncertainty, fuelled by the man's familiarity and the alertness to danger Mulligan had drilled into him, warning 'the war is barely over.' He explained that he had only arrived, and was just getting his bearings, annoyed for sounding so defensive, like an intruder caught in the act. The stranger interrogated him gently, each answer sparking another question, until he had established that Kennedy was part of an Irish delegation to Zimbabwe, led by Senator Cahill, accompanied by another civil servant and an aid co-ordinator. The American appeared satisfied. 'So, we're in the same game. I always knew I could pick out another spook a mile away.'

Kennedy spluttered in protest and the laughing American held out his hand.

'It's OK. You don't have to convince me. Everyone here thinks we're spooks anyway. I'm Jack Clay, nothing to Cassius, Nairobi Embassy of the United States. They sent me down from the office in Kenya to do a recon. They thought I might blend in better.'

Kennedy shook his hand confidently, more at ease to be dealing with another diplomat.

'As you'll soon figure out, I don't blend in at all.' The American accompanied this statement with a sweep of his hand, taking in his surroundings. Kennedy was perplexed, but Jack Clay glanced at his watch, making a show of suddenly remembering an appointment and took a step away.

'Are you guys meeting Mugabe?' He waited, preparing to evaluate Kennedy's answer.

'Nothing's arranged.' Then, afraid he had given too much away, Kennedy added, 'Yet.'

'I hope you have better luck than me. This Mugabe guy seems to think he's the shooting scarlet pimpernel of the African revolution. Two weeks later and we have no sign of getting an audience with the great one.' At that Jack Clay stepped away and with a wave of his hand said, 'See you around, Tom. We can grab a beer in Meikles.'

Kennedy waited at the street corner, feeling foolish and exposed. If the American had asked him what he had had for breakfast, he would have told him. He hoped his little encounter had not been noticed by anyone. Losing confidence in his ability to handle this strange place, he retreated to the hotel. He had hardly managed to get twenty yards on his African adventure. Waiting for the lift, he asked himself just how much of a coincidence was it to bump into an

American embassy official? Why did he have a vague sense of being set up? What would Mulligan say? Should he tell him?

Patricia Lynch was not taken in by the general peacefulness. Except for the incident at the airport, there were few signs of the violence that had been an everyday part of this country's life. But she knew how deceptive the cities in war-torn countries could be. Usually in the struggles in Africa, the cities were the last to be affected, protected by tacit agreements between the warring factions to keep these jewels as the winners' spoils while they settled their scores in the isolated villages. She sat on the edge of the bed, too muddled to sleep. Now that she was here, what exactly was she going to do next? Already she could see herself returning home, the same questions left unanswered.

She had just finished her nursing training when the Mercy Hospital offered her a permanent post. The fact that her mother knew the matron probably had something to do with it, but to her credit she had won third place in a class of ninety other girls. To mark the occasion, her boyfriend of three years proposed to her. Everything was falling so neatly into place. She loved making the arrangements for the wedding, the enhanced status of being engaged, trying to imagine what it would be like to have their own house, their own space where they could do what they liked.

Could you spare just one month of your life?

It was an appeal for nursing volunteers to go to Biafra, described as the greatest humanitarian disaster of the sixties. As soon as she saw it she knew that she must do this one thing in her life before she settled down. Her fiancé was supportive. She told her parents it was her way of thanking God. They were supportive. The matron was displeased at this disruption to her rosters, but could not say 'no' to the will of God, particularly when the poor Biafrans were Catholics, the stories from the Irish priests feeding a frenzy of concern.

In her first day in the refugee camp three children perished in her work area. One of them died in her arms as his mother silently pleaded into Patricia's face. The emaciated Biafran woman watched Patricia cry tears she herself was too dehydrated to shed, tears landing on her child's forehead, trickling into the hollow of his right eye, still open, still staring. The numbed mother waited mournfully until Patricia stopped crying. Then she took her baby and wrapped him in her flimsy shawl, enfolding the body back into her own and walked out of the camp. At no stage had she spoken. She had offered Patricia her child, and now she took it back again. There was no hint of criticism in the woman's actions, just a deep despair that there was no one who could save her son from death.

The pattern continued with the numbers arriving at the camp increasing each day. Patricia tried to triage the children without holding them, to assess should they be moved to another part of the camp and fed in the hope of saving their lives, or if they were too far gone to help. Some were already dead. After six days she walked out the gate, following the dirt track against the flow of human misery fleeing the savagery of the civil war and the indiscriminate death sentences of famine. She did not know why or where she was going, bareheaded under the midday sun, ignored by all who passed her.

Then she saw him, the man who had caused all this misery, standing in the middle of the road, his fancy uniform buttons glistening in the sun. He was too busy shouting orders to notice her approaching until she was next to him. When he turned towards her, she drew back her hand at full arm's length and slapped him across the face. She felt her shoulders being grabbed, her wrists tightly held. She did not care what was done to her; they could kill her there and then. When she had finished kicking and screaming, the grips were loosened and she collapsed on the ground, curling into the foetal position, sobbing in huge heaves, unable to control the tears flowing down her cheeks, gagging from the snot running into her throat.

The man she had hit appeared to be standing over her. She

wanted him to kill her, to finish this nightmare. He called to someone. She heard the thud of boots on the parched earth, could feel their vibration on the hard soil as they came close to her head. She flinched, waiting for the kick that was about to be delivered. She felt hands on her ankles and shoulders. Then she had the sensation of floating, up, up. When she was released, she did not fall. Instead, her whole body was being supported. The angels had come and were taking her to heaven.

Even before Patricia opened her eyes, everything was familiar: the smell of ammonia; the distinct, hollow sound of aluminium on tile; and the measured, efficient voices. She knew what she would see when she dared to peek. She was in a white envelope, the sheet up to her nose almost blending into the whiteness of the ceiling. But there was a large propeller overhead, going slowly round and round. Now, that was a surprise! A uniform came close to her. She tilted her head, trying to figure out which of her friends had come to take care of her. Another surprise was the smiling black face of a young woman at the top of the starched whiteness. She raised her head to take in this view of a ward. The ten beds were little islands on the shiny tiled surface, the nurses gliding about. Her training had taught her to recognise the busy air preceding a doctor's rounds, the nurses waking patients, fluffing their pillows, encouraging them to appear better. A very big man, his white coat flapping like a sheet, came towards her bed, smiling.

'So, how is our stretcher case today?' he teased lightly.

Was this the same man on whom she had blamed the horrors of the refugee camp? She wanted to curl up again and hide under the sheet in embarrassment. But he smilingly confirmed her suspicions, treating the incident as a joke. 'We need some light relief in these situations,' he informed her in a good-humoured voice.

He explained that they had been obliged to keep the hospital services totally separate from the refugee camp, afraid that a facility that had taken twenty years to put in place would be wiped out overnight by an unmanageable influx of refugees. The day Patricia had attacked him he had been on one of his regular visits to the outskirts of the camp, trying to identify those who were well enough to benefit from hospital treatment

'Each day, I stand there in my Red Cross uniform and play God, selecting who might live and who will die, As a doctor, working with scarce resources, this is something I have to tolerate. But it does not make it any easier.'

At first he adamantly refused to even discuss letting her work at the hospital. It was obvious her nursing training in Ireland had not prepared her for this daily toll of human misery. But her appeal to the sister matron, always wanting more help, was promptly accepted.

As the only doctor, he doubled as house surgeon, and they worked together in the operating theatre from before dawn until late morning, when the heat of the day made the masks and gowns unbearable. Most of the surgery was straightforward: removing appendices, tonsils and, sometimes, amputations of a gangrenous finger or toe. The more complicated cases could not be dealt with, necessitating decisions to send people home to await their death.

Within weeks they became lovers, and Patricia was never sure afterwards just how pure her motives were for staying on at the hospital. The aid agency that had brought her to West Africa had lost interest in her, relieved they were not bringing her home in a straitjacket.

Her family's letters told her how proud they were to know their daughter had answered God's call when they listened to the priests, Sunday after Sunday, exhorting them not to forget the starving Biafran Catholics, victims of the pagan Nigerian government. The letters from her fiancé were different. When her replies became sparser, she could read the frustration in his short notes. 'The builder says we must decide on the plans within the month if we want the house ready on time.' 'On time for what?' was her first reaction and then she felt a small pang of guilt, unable to identify with the girl who had set her heart on the 'house on the hill'. It all seemed so far away now; a dream she could not connect to; she could not imagine a life before her lover.

'I think I am more needed in my own country.'

Patricia raised herself on her elbow, her face over his. 'Are you going into the bush?'

He laughed gently at the innocence of her question. 'My years in university in Canada have ill-prepared me for life in the bush. Even here, I need the cocoon of a hospital to survive. I will return to Bulawayo and try to get work in the main hospital. If my skills are needed by the freedom fighters, I'm sure there's plenty of ways that I can be of assistance.'

They had discussed the struggle for democracy in Rhodesia enough for her to appreciate what was at stake. A year before she had been only vaguely aware of what was happening, had understood it more in terms of a political stand-off between the Rhodesian whites and the British government. The war between black and white in the Southern African bush had never really crossed her mind. She was not alone in this ignorance. For many, this was just another hidden conflict in Africa, being waged away from the TV cameras preoccupying the living rooms of the West with the war in Vietnam.

It was an armed struggle doomed to fail, according to the general discussions in the hospital canteen. Even their native African colleagues insisted that the rebels' Marxist motivations would only damage the quality of life of the majority population in Rhodesia, probably the best-fed and best-housed black people in Africa. Her lover listened patiently to these points, always coming back to one core argument. Freedom. Democracy. The recent history of who had cultivated Rhodesia was not the issue he would say. 'Three per cent of the population are white; they control ninety five percent of the wealth. Let us share it equally and then there need not be any bloodshed. Let each man, each person, have a vote.'

Patricia stayed on the fringes of the animated discussions, feeling ignorant amid the wide-ranging knowledge of the Red Cross corps, drawn from Sweden, Norway, England, India and the new African countries of Zambia and Kenya. Everyone seemed so knowledgeable, not just about what was happening in Rhodesia, but about African and world politics that they comfortably carved up into labelled sections: East, West; North, South; Capitalist, Marxist; Democratic, Dictatorship; Rich, Poor. First, second and third worlds, sounding like different planets.

'I sometimes get so confused. Everyone here is so opinionated I'm afraid to open my mouth. But even your fellow Africans are saying that the Rhodesian guerrillas do not have popular support. Is it all doomed to failure?'

He sat on the edge of the bed, facing away from her. She knew from the way he hunched his broad shoulders that now, privately, he was less confident of the position he had so eloquently held in the canteen.

Eventually she had to speak the words. 'Could they be right?'

Momentarily lost in his own internal debate and then, suddenly relaxing, he lay down beside her, smiling.

'And you, my young Irish lass, have you forgotten about Mr Pearse and Mr Connolly and how little support they had in 1916?'

They had arranged to meet for lunch, and the three of them sat in the formal restaurant waiting for Cahill, critiquing Meikles Hotel. Mulligan and Patricia scoffed at its colonial stuffiness, but Tom Kennedy insisted they were just cynics.

'I like restaurants with style and service. And there seems to be a bit more service than I got from the phone company,' he told them. 'I've been trying to ring home as we think Ronan's coming down with something, but they tell me the international lines are down.'

Making conversation, Mulligan wanted to know, 'What do operators mean when they say "the lines are down". Have wires fallen to the ground somewhere?' They amused themselves speculating about the phrase, killing time as they waited for the senator. Mulligan tried Cahill's phone from the dining room and was surprised to find it engaged. They dawdled at the table, the evening-suited waiter hovering uncertainly nearby. Mulligan tried Cahill's line again. Still engaged.

'I think our good senator must have fallen asleep and taken his phone off the hook,' Mulligan told the others, 'I'll give him a shout.'

'Very commendable. It would not do for our "good senator" to go hungry.' Patricia laughed, taking the edge off her remark.

'You're the worst type of cynic of all, Mizzz Lynch. A young one. And how did you guess that I just want to give his penthouse pad the once-over?'

When the lift reached the top floor he had to go to the end of the corridor, up a short flight of stairs and across the open roof under a short, canopied walkway to the penthouse, sitting in splendid isolation. From the shape of the wall-slated structure, Mulligan estimated that it must be four times as big as an average hotel room. He had his knuckle raised to knock on the door when he heard Cahill's voice. 'Absolutely. Absolutely.'

From the one-sided sounds, Mulligan knew that the senator was on the phone, and his remaining diplomatic instincts warned him to get away from the door without alerting Cahill to his presence. More 'aha, aha' from Cahill in agreement with the caller and then he answered in a loud, confident voice. 'Have no worries. I promise you we'll get it sorted. That's why I'm here.'

Mulligan went to his own room and again phoned Cahill: on the third attempt, he answered.

'I just wanted to remind you about lunch, Senator.'

'I'll be right down. I must have fallen asleep.' Cahill repeated the excuse to the others, half-yawning into his fist to emphasise its veracity. Patricia Lynch said something about long haul travelling being so exhausting, while Mulligan privately speculated, if the international lines were down, who in Rhodesia could Cahill have been talking to?

'I'm going to Bulawayo for the weekend.' Patricia sounded casual, sipping her coffee. Cahill said sharply, 'Bulawayo must be a few hundred miles away, why, it could even be a war zone.'

Patricia did not reply. Cahill redirected his ire at Mulligan. 'Is this in the plan?' His exasperated tone silently adding, what is this woman up to now? Mulligan's shrug indicated what Cahill knew. Patricia Lynch was not an official of the Department, so she was not answerable to Mulligan or the senator.

'Why Bulawayo?' Mulligan's prompt was gentle. He could sense her deep unease and felt it was probably apparent to the others.

'Well,' she said, speaking directly to Mulligan, playing for time, 'as you know, John, the war very likely had a different impact there. I think it's important to make an on-the-ground assessment. If I go today, I can be back early on Monday and will not miss many meetings.'

Mulligan decided to help her out and agreed without further interrogation, realising that he was not the only one with another agenda.

Lunch was long over and they were sitting about, waiting for an opportunity to extricate themselves from one another. It was a one-time familiar situation that Mulligan had not experienced in some years, having been cut off from trips abroad in his Departmental purgatory. Overseas travel threw people together who normally would not spend two minutes in each other's company. The more foreign the place, by language, culture or security, the more the travellers were locked into uneasy alliances. Now as they sat in Meikles' almost empty dining room, three men and one woman from different backgrounds, of different ages, with a protocol awkwardness thrown in for good measure, Mulligan worried how were they going to get through the next five days. He was regretting arranging to arrive on a Saturday to give them a chance to get their bearings.

The waiter hurried towards them, followed by a small man with an overweight puffiness, exaggerated by a suit two sizes too tight for him. As he reached the table, the waiter stepped aside and the white stranger approached and stopped.

'Mr Mulligan?' His look questioned the two older men, ignoring Tom Kennedy, obviously too junior in his view to be the one he wanted to meet. Mulligan rose, extending his hand. 'Judge Bradshaw.' They shook hands quickly, business-like.

'My apologies for being unable to return your calls, Mr Mulligan, but' and Bradshaw threw a glance around the dining room, 'it is difficult to conduct business by phone these days.'

'Senator,' Mulligan said formally, pausing to ensure Cahill was listening, 'I would like to introduce one of the leading figures in Salisbury legal circles, Judge Robert Bradshaw.'

Bradshaw sat at the edge of his chair, leaning towards Cahill and Mulligan. 'I'm very pleased you're here Senator Cahill.' He spoke in a low voice, glancing sporadically over his shoulder. 'The Irish community in Rhodesia is honoured that you will be taking such an interest in our future.'

Cahill ignored the perplexed Mulligan and gave his undivided attention to the anxious judge. Bradshaw was encouraged and determined to continue, not waiting for Cahill to reply. 'But it's best not to talk business here. "The walls have ears," as they say. I've taken the liberty of arranging dinner this evening at the Salisbury Club, where there will be a number of people who are keen to meet you. I hope you gentlemen will also be free to attend.' He gestured towards Mulligan and Kennedy, confirming their inclusion.

Patricia picked up and noisily replaced her empty coffee cup, but Bradshaw continued to behave like she did not exist. Even Cahill was becoming uncomfortable with the ongoing discourtesy. Having delivered his invitation, Bradshaw relaxed.

'Excuse my lack of manners, gentlemen, let me buy you a beer to welcome you to Rhodesia.' He raised his right hand and clicked his fingers. 'May I recommend the only local brew the European stomach can tolerate.'

Finally, Bradshaw considered Patricia, as if seeing her for the first time. 'Oh, excuse me, Senator,' he said ingratiatingly at Cahill, 'but I cannot extend the invitation to your secretary. You see, since its foundation, the Salisbury Club has been reserved for "men only".'

'And… "whites only".' Patricia jumped up, her cheeks burning, throwing her napkin on the table in Cahill's direction and left the dining room without looking back. Bradshaw shrugged in feigned dismay, 'How did she guess?'

Mulligan was pleased to see that even Cahill blushed.

'Did you want something?' The waiter had witnessed the whole episode, and was very deliberately speaking coldly to Bradshaw. No routine 'sir' in his question.

'Bring me four beers.' Bradshaw had obviously noted the calculated insult and was trying to get his own back. As the waiter walked away, Mulligan called after him, 'Excuse me. Please! But I will have a coke.'

The man stopped and, addressing himself directly at Mulligan, half bowed and said, 'Yes. Sir.'

Mulligan did not wait for the judge's driver to hurry around to open his door as well. Despite the dark, he could sense the surrounding opulence from the amount of shrubbery hiding the houses and the sentry boxes inside the closed gates. He felt uncomfortable in his suit in the warm evening. The driver moved aside as they went up the steps towards the double glass doors, one of which was opened inwards by a tall black man in a bellboy uniform and hat. A very well polished, discreet, brass plate, reflecting the white streetlights, said simply 'The Salisbury Club.' Bradshaw came into the hall, flushed from drink and full of self-importance.

'Senator Cahill, gentlemen, welcome to the Salisbury Club.' He shook hands only with Cahill and, taking his elbow, guided him into the centre of the large tiled hall. 'We are honoured to have such a distinguished guest from the "old sod".' With a small flourish, he added, 'Our visitors' book.' He presented a gold fountain pen to Cahill and gestured towards a large, ledger-style book sitting open on a writing desk. Cahill was soaking up the flattery. When he had signed, Bradshaw put the pen back in his pocket and led Cahill down a dimly lit corridor. Opening a solid door with African animals carved out of its panels, the judge confided, 'We have taken the liberty of using one of the smaller private rooms.' At that he stepped back and, with a grand sweep of his arm, indicated they should precede him into a large room lit by a huge chandelier, sparkling as the warm air from the open windows jiggled the cut glass droplets. In the middle of the "smaller" room was a table covered with a white cloth, silver cutlery glistening in the reflections from the shining glasses. At the far end three men, drinks in hand, awaited their visitors. Bradshaw guided Cahill towards them. 'Gerry, I would like to introduce members of the real club in Salisbury, the Irish club.'

'Gentlemen, this is Senator Gerry Cahill.' Bradshaw was acting like he had caught a prize animal. A very baby-faced young man, with a purple waistcoat below his white dog collar, stepped forward.

'And this is His Lordship, William O'Brien, our recently-appointed bishop.' He was the youngest bishop Mulligan had ever seen, and he was curious to know how sympathetic to the black struggle had his predecessor been, thinking ruefully that someone in Rome had obviously bet on the wrong side when assessing where the Catholic Church should align itself and was surely now regretting their policy of disownment of guerrilla sympathisers.

'Sean Kirby runs the only local rag that matters, but we try not to hold that against him.' The newspaperman was taller than Mulligan, but slightly stooped and gaunt-faced. Gerry Cahill warmly worked through the introductions.

'And, of course, you know Mr Eamonn Doran,' Bradshaw laughed.

'Good to see you again, Gerry,' the last man said, taking Cahill's hand and gripping it with both of his.

'What you may not know about this man, Gerry, is what an important role he is playing in the National Farmers' Union,' Bradshaw said as Cahill continued shaking hands with Doran. 'Why, we may even have a future Minister for Agriculture in our presence.'

Eamonn Doran laughingly protested as Cahill cuffed him playfully on the shoulder. When Mulligan and Kennedy were greeted in turn, Mulligan gave Doran special consideration, attempting to read who he was: how did he know Cahill so well?

Making small talk about their flight and the hotel, the two parties were trying to groove into place. It was the newspaperman who decided to break the ice.

'Mr Mulligan? John?' He said it loudly enough for all to turn towards him. Smiling at Mulligan, he stroked his face in a play of checking how well he had shaved himself. 'We are gaining an appreciation of just how cut off we have been from the "outside world" when we see such a hirsute senior civil servant. We thought beards were the preserve of beatniks.'

Mulligan laughed heartily, giving the lead to the others. Cahill and Eamonn Doran conspiratorially toasted each other. Cahill was given the seat at the top of the table, flanked by Bradshaw and Eamonn Doran. Mulligan sat next to Doran, wanting to stay close to what was happening. The bishop, too green to have assumed the status of his position, and Tom Kennedy waited for the others to be seated and then took the remaining seats, facing each other.

The headwaiter nervously shifted from foot to foot in the side doorway, waiting to be summoned, the remainder of his staff somewhere discreetly off-stage until they were required.

The menus had specially printed covers.

Dinner at the Salisbury Club
in honour of
Mr Gerard Cahill
Member of Seanad Éireann
on his visit to Rhodesia.
Saturday, May 24th, 1980.

There was a lot of talk about Ireland, Mulligan and Cahill doing most of the answering. Cahill was in a gregarious mood and passed questions to Tom Kennedy for his opinion. This pattern continued throughout the elaborately presented meal, a main course of prime Rhodesian beef introduced as the pride of the farming community, the most successful in Africa. During the lulls in discussion, Mulligan established that Eamonn Doran was Cahill's brother-in-law. He made no attempt to hide his surprise, and Doran was amused that Mulligan had been kept in the dark for so long. That old cute whoor of his brother-in-law never would tell his right hand what the left was doing, he boasted to Mulligan, who grimaced in agreement.

A box of cigars was placed beside Cahill. The headwaiter watched as the two servants deposited brandies in front of each diner, except Mulligan, and then shepherded them from the room, closing the door from the outside. A tinkling of a glass brought the focus back on the journalist, Seán Kirby. He stood up, marking the resumption of formalities.

'Senator. We are, indeed, honoured that you have come so soon to Rhodesia to see for yourself the state of affairs we now find ourselves in and what is now at stake as we move into this period of…of adjustment. You have come to the jewel in what was once the crown of southern Africa. A jewel in a tattered crown of Zam…bia. Bot…swana.' His voice was full of derision, lips curling even further downward. 'And, now, it appears we are about to have Zim…bab…we.' He considered the incongruity of the name and then laughed dismissively. 'If only it were just the names that change.' He sipped his brandy. 'Senator. The success of Rhodesia is built on one key ingredient, the farming, the white Rhodesian farming-community who have irrigated these hostile lands to create the breadbasket of Africa.'

'Hear, hear,' the other locals agreed, except for the bishop who cautiously watched the proceedings. Mulligan had overheard him telling Kennedy he had only recently arrived in Salisbury, adding 'I'm working on my tan.' Deciphering this as code for, 'I'm not the same as these settlers,' Mulligan sympathised now with O'Brien's increasing embarrassment.

'We know, Senator, you will be able to see at first-hand tomorrow just how successful farmers like Eamonn have been. You will also see how well off his farm workers are, how well fed they are compared to the so-called farmers in Zam…bia, Bot…swana.' The disdain in his voice and on his lips was even more pronounced, the alcohol and looming gravity of the new political situation not allowing any room for subtlety. Cahill watched the newspaperman intently, little nods silently signalling his agreement.

'We ask you, Senator, and your government, as Irishmen to Irishmen, that you use your special position in the EEC to impress on your European colleagues that Mugabe, and his side-kick Nkomo, must be told...be warned...the Rhodesian farms must remain in the hands of their rightful owners. Otherwise, Rhodesia will be lost to us all and the whole population will be poorer for it.'

There were more mutterings of 'Hear, hear.' Kirby swished the brandy around his glass and toasted their support. Raising his hand, the judge added, 'And, when you get to meet with Mis...ter, Com...rade, Prime Minister, Mugabe, we would appreciate you conveying to him how seriously Europe is taking his promises that the white community will be respected as we all repair the damage from the past. The law must be upheld.' The judge, chuffed that he had got in a word for the remainder of the white Rhodesian population and for law and order, added, 'Senator?'

As Cahill spoke, Mulligan studied the eclectic gathering of Rhodesians, trying to accept that the past was over and unable to come to terms with the future.

What if I were to die here? Far from home. Who would have foreseen when I was leaving school at eighteen that I would meet my end in the middle of Africa? That this little piece of machinery would fall out of the sky? Giving us a minute, or would it be less, to do what? Pray? Probably. Would my life really flash before me? Would I remember the parts from my mad drinking days that I don't even remember now? These morbid thoughts crowded into Mulligan's head as the little plane circled over the African countryside. Andrew Doran, Cahill's nephew, was at the controls: a young man, hardly twenty, expertly in charge. It was his father who suggested that he take their visitors for a tour of the farm. Mulligan had assumed they were going for a drive and was reluctant to back out when Andrew led them around the enormous cowsheds towards a four-seater

Cessna single-engine aircraft. Cahill sat in front next to his nephew and Mulligan and Kennedy had the two rear seats. Mulligan had never been in an aircraft so small, and he was immediately reminded of the interior of his first car, a fourth-hand Volkswagen, christened the 'craic chariot' by Kate as they used it on summer weekends to flee Dublin, chasing the music and the magical festiveness of west Clare and Connemara.

'How big did you say it was?' Kennedy leaned forward and shouted into Andrew Doran's ear.

'Oh, a few thousand acres.' Andrew Doran threw the figure out in what Mulligan felt was a feigned nonchalance. Was the young man evading giving a specific answer, had he perhaps become self-conscious about owning thousands of acres of land? They were flying over some of it now and he pointed out the irrigated soil, stark green rectangles sitting on the red-brown African landscape.

'Cotton' he shouted above the noise of the engine. 'The maize is over there.' He stretched his left arm straight out. They ranged over what appeared to be miles of cultivation. 'We don't do tobacco any more. Dad still talks about it, but I hardly remember when.'

The little plane swung sharply to the right, leaving the farmland, crossing over the bush with its isolated pockets of vegetation exuding an aura of a deserted landscape. There were not enough trees together to make up even a small wood, and from the air they appeared skimpy, clinging to survival: skeletal branches praying for rain. A village came into view. Andrew brought the plane lower so that they could better see the little cluster of mud huts, smoke streeling from the holes in the conical straw roofs of two of them. There was no other sign of life.

'It's like stepping back in time,' Kennedy said aloud, to no one in particular, clearly enjoying every minute of his first visit to Africa. It was he who had jumped at Eamonn Doran's invitation, anxious to see more than just the city of Salisbury. Mulligan had the impression that Cahill had not intended for his brother-in-law to also invite them to the farm, but the situation went outside his control in Doran's bonhomie.

'Parts of Africa have not changed in hundreds of years,' Andrew shouted over his shoulder to Tom Kennedy. 'Dad is always on about the way Rhodesian farmers have modernised this country, in spite of itself. I'm sure he did a bit of boasting about our new milking parlour when he was showing you around,' Andrew laughed.

'He sure did.' Mulligan said it in a jocose, wistful way, underlining the fact that Eamonn Doran had prattled on about his new recording system, enabling him to precisely tell the yield from each of his six hundred and twelve cows.

'We wanted to know how he remembered all the cows' names,' Cahill said to his nephew, laughing again at the little joke he had made when his brother-in-law told them the size of his herd. But the joke was lost on Andrew Doran, who had never even been to Ireland, having no understanding of the small size of Irish holdings, where the farmer would have names for his twenty or thirty milking-cows and a little story about every animal, giving each a character of her own.

When they touched down, Eamonn Doran came to meet them carrying a tray of cold beer and iced tea for Mulligan. 'For the Irishman who doesn't drink,' he said ceremoniously, but all Mulligan could hear was, 'For the man with a drink problem.'

Kennedy and Mulligan watched from under the shade of a large, straw umbrella as Andrew prepared the barbecue. Cahill had gone indoors to catch up on old times with his sister, Mary. The warmth of their reunion had struck Mulligan. She was at least ten years older than Cahill and called him 'my little Gerry' as she hugged him, held him at arm's length to size him up and then embraced him again and again. Cahill was warm towards her in turn and kept telling her how like their mother she had become. It was a side to Cahill that Mulligan had not seen before, a tender side that he was disinclined to give him credit for in his antipathy. Mary Cahill Doran had not seen her younger brother in the fifteen years of UDI and cried and laughed and jokingly called him 'Senator', testing the important-sounding word.

'Imagine how proud mammy and daddy would have been,' she

said nostalgically.

'Being a senator is nothing, it's these fellas who really run the country.' Cahill indicated Mulligan and Kennedy, anxious to introduce them so that her effusiveness could be deflated. Mary Doran pressed their hands heartily, welcoming them as close friends of her brother rather than happenstance travelling companions. Mulligan liked this warm, motherly woman who appeared unchanged by her years in Africa, first in South Africa and the last twenty-two in Rhodesia. They had not liked South Africa, she told them as they had tea and sandwiches 'just to keep them going' in the dark, heavily-furnitured sitting room. They had not liked the way the blacks were treated in South Africa, she said reflectively, shaking her head to reprimand the memories of apartheid. 'For heaven's sake, I can visit any of our senior farm workers' houses and sit down and talk to them as neighbours. We're on first name terms. Andrew, and his sister Breda, who is now at the teachers' training college in Salisbury, have played with our workers' children as friends all their lives.'

Later, watching her son turn huge slabs of steak on the barbecue, chatting to the black woman setting the table, Mulligan thought about what she had said, sincere in her regard for the farm workers, her dislike of South Africa's apartheid. He was in a philosophical mood after surviving the trip in the small aircraft, taking a large view of the world.

'A word from the wise, Tom,' he mused aloud and then sipped his iced tea, pausing for effect, leaving Kennedy waiting for him to continue with one of his famous pronouncements. 'Don't let anyone tell you the war in Rhodesia was about freedom, or democracy, or black and white.' Mulligan looked around the farm, tilting his head towards the distant horizon. 'This war was about land.'

Even the flies seemed to have given up in the Sunday-afternoon heat and the only sounds were the lowing of the cows. The sky was clear blue but for some wispy white clouds on the western horizon. The heat was dryer than what Mulligan remembered of Zambia, with this part of Rhodesia's altitude lifting it out of the general African humidity. Mulligan could not catch what they were saying, but it was obvious from their banter that the young African woman and Andrew were comfortable with each other, proof indeed of Mary Doran's point. Listening to the peaceful domesticity of the food being prepared, Mulligan dozed, happy to be back in Africa, happy with the arrangements he had made for later that evening.

He was tired after the two-hour drive in the cold dawn; all were silent in the jeep as they rushed across the smooth, tarmacadamed roads out of Salisbury into the emptiness of the countryside. Despite the lateness of the finish in the Salisbury Club, where Cahill's over-enthusiastic support for the Rhodesian white farmers went far beyond Irish government policy, Eamonn Doran had insisted they get going at first light as he was anxious to have them back in the city before dark. About an hour outside Salisbury he stopped at a small, red stone church and, without consulting anybody, led the way into mass. They were late. The African priest's sermon on "the meek shall inherit the earth" was greeted by a vigorous "amen" from the mainly black congregation. Mulligan kept his head bowed while Cahill, Kennedy and Doran joined the queue for communion, reminding himself of his old catechism doctrine that only God knows what is in each man's soul.

'Mr Mulligan,' Andrew called, 'Fatima wants to know how does Ireland stop the seas from drowning it?' The young African woman laughed and shyly busied herself at the table.

'That, Andrew, is a six-marker,' Mulligan replied, laughing in turn, buying a little time as he searched for words to describe the sea to someone in a landlocked country.

'In fact, I wouldn't mind knowing the answer to that myself,' Andrew added and he and the woman laughed again. Fatima kept her back turned to the two visitors as she continued preparing the salads, too shy or status-conscious to join directly in the conversation.

'Some parts of it do get covered from time to time,' Mulligan said, but realised this answer would probably only add to whatever mistaken impression she, and possibly Andrew, had of the sea.

'What do you think, Tom?'

Kennedy laughed in turn, realising he was being put on the spot by Mulligan. He had grown up with the Atlantic coast framed in the back windows of his mother's bed and breakfast. The ever-changing seascapes, colours varying from dark grey to blue and green, sometimes even in the course of a few minutes, were just something he assumed was part of life. 'Ireland is like a plateau sitting on the sea bed, rising up out of the water.'

The servant said something to Andrew and they both laughed. Andrew did not pass on her comments to the visiting Irishmen.

'I think we will have to come up with a better explanation,' Mulligan said, loud enough for all to hear, acknowledging the inadequacy of their efforts. From the direction of the house they could hear voices. When the others joined them, Cahill seemed particularly subdued.

'Andrew, the steaks are mouth-watering,' his father exuberated, rubbing his hands, wanting to re-ignite their spirits. 'And, as always, Fatima, you have prepared the best salads in Rhodesia.'

The African woman beamed, pleased at the recognition in front of the white visitors and gave the hint of a curtsy towards her employer.

Eamonn Doran insisted that Cahill sit at the head of the long trestle table, built to seat twenty or so people. Cahill's sister and her husband were on either side of him, with the two civil servants next to them. Andrew placed his plate at the opposite end, away from the others, but did not sit down, opting instead to take care of the barbecue. The table was under a shed without walls, really just a galvanised roof sitting on stilts, giving welcome shelter from the afternoon sun.

Fatima checked to make sure everyone had enough salads and gathered the huge steaks from Andrew for distribution. After a little jokey apology, seeking his guests' forgiveness for breaking Ireland's trade sanctions against South Africa, Doran produced two bottles of red wine. All except Mulligan let him fill their glasses, with Mulligan changing from iced tea to coke. Andrew was not invited to have a drink, and Mulligan assumed he was designated with the job of getting them back to Salisbury in one piece.

'Well Mr Mulligan, I won't be as abstemious as you. I think a woman is perfectly entitled to celebrate seeing her younger brother after all these years.'

'I can think of no better reason for celebration.'

Mary Cahill Doran raised her full glass in response to Mulligan's gallantry, pointedly ignoring her husband.

Conversation around the table was sparse, people concentrating on their food to make up for the fact that they had little to say to each other. Halfway through the meal, at the end of a particularly long silence, Mulligan heard Kennedy say, 'I'm sure you must be thankful the war is over?' They all paused simultaneously, Kennedy's question hanging in the stillness.

The only sound was Fatima singing to herself as she continued tidying the nearby salad table.

Eamonn Doran answered. 'The war was a tragedy for us and for Rhodesia; it should never have happened. It was a bloody nuisance, every inch of the way.' He emphasised the last words by drumming the table with his right fingertips. 'A bunch of communists have been allowed to bring this country almost to its knees,' he added, turning to his brother-in-law for support, obviously trying to steer away from opening a discussion with his wife.

Cahill wiped his lips with his napkin and then took another drink of wine. 'Yes, I must say I feel-'

'God knows, we should have negotiated from the start.' Mary Doran cut across her brother, speaking defiantly at her husband. Her voice was hollow, weary of repeating the same point in what was obviously a well-worn argument between the couple. Mulligan watched Cahill with his knife and fork hovering above his plate as he analysed his sister, trying to come to terms with the depth of pain contorting her appearance.

'Too many lives have been lost.' At that her face slackened into an older resemblance of the woman who had met them earlier. The tears flowed down her cheeks. Eamonn Doran's eyes filled up and he abruptly left the table. The two civil servants examined their food, unable to look into the depths of a mother's loss. Cahill placed his hand firmly around his sister's clenched fist.

'I am really sorry,' Tom Kennedy stressed every word, uncertain as to what terrible grief he had unlocked, 'to have upset you.'

'The senator had not confided in us,' Mulligan added, silently saying to Cahill, this is where your lifetime policy of not letting your left hand know what your right hand is doing has got us.

'My brother was one of the first Rhodesian officers to die in the cross border operations. On a hot-pursuit mission into Mozambique, in fact.' Andrew Doran spoke directly to his uncle, who was carefully taking stock of him from the opposite end of the table. 'I'm sure the subtlety of my phraseology has not been lost on you, Uncle Gerry. Note, I did not say "soldier", but "officer". My brother Edward was one of the first whites to be killed in the war.' He let them consider this information. His mother blew her nose. The tears had stopped flowing and she appeared to have partly recovered.

'Young Eddie loved Rhodesia with his very bones,' she said to no one in particular, tracing the rim of her plate with the second finger of her left hand, dabbing at her eyes and nose with the crumpled tissue in her right fist. 'He loved this farm. The people working on it. Before the war "escalated" he and Fatima's brother, Reg,' she spoke towards the woman, who bowed her head, acknowledging the mention of her brother, 'and another of our farm workers, Ken Matambira, would disappear together into the bush for days, hunting and fishing. They called themselves the three musketeers.'

'I used to beg to go with them,' Andrew spoke wistfully, catching his mother's nostalgic tone, 'but I was too young.'

'When Andrew was old enough to go into the bush, it was not for fun.' Until he spoke, no one had noticed Eamonn Doran returning. He moved now behind his son, placing one hand on his shoulder.

'I should add,' Mary Doran said, turning again towards the African woman, the pride rising in her voice, 'our Eddie and Fatima's Reg and Ken died together. Side by side.'

Fatima moved closer to the table but stopped, kept back by an invisible barrier. As she turned away, her shoulders heaved and she covered her face with her apron.

'They say it is the most noble thing. To die for your country.' Cahill placed his hands on the table, palms upwards, acknowledging the emptiness of his remark. The two civil servants mumbled agreement, unable to add anything.

'This is not our country, Uncle Gerry. This country belongs to the Shona and Matabele people.' His father squeezed his shoulder, but Andrew was not going to be deterred.

'I was born here and I believed everyone respected our right to be here. Since I was eighteen years old, I have spent months of every year in the bush fighting for that right. I have been part of a war that no one wants to hear about now. No one wants to know what we did to the other side. What they did to us. No one knows who committed the first atrocity, or who was retaliating. I was one white officer with thirty black soldiers. I believed what we were told, that the rebels were only a tiny number of Marxist troublemakers. That the majority of the black people appreciated the way we had made this country what it is. That Mugabe and Nkomo had no rightful place in Rhodesian democratic elections.'

Eamonn Doran was stock-still, silent, head-bent, a hand on his son's shoulder.

'And now the people have spoken. They have made their choice for Marxist Mugabe and his fat friend Joshua Nkomo. Why, maybe even Fatima voted against us, but that's a question no one wants to ask. In the same way that we did not want to ask where did Fatima's younger brother go when he disappeared.' Andrew Doran combatively regarded his audience, challenging someone to contradict him. He glanced at the servant, then back to the white people, changing his mind about where he would direct his question, wanting to spare her any further difficulty.

'Did he go into the bush to fight against me?' Andrew appeared to be genuinely curious to know the answer.

'I have been deceived. We all have. My brother gave his life for this country. I gave my teenage years. When I should have been just having a good time, listening to pop music, I was a bloody soldier: a teenage, army officer. Doing what soldiers do…' He faltered, seeming to become aware that he had taken centre stage, not wanting the limelight any longer. He moved towards the barbecue, 'And you know what soldiers do.'

Fatima joined him, their backs to the others, elbows almost touching as they worked together, whispering, recovering the closeness between them.

The equilibrium of the meal had been partially restored before they left. When Mulligan said they regretted not being able to include a trip to Victoria Falls on their itinerary, Cahill muttered encouragement. Turning the conversation around, Mulligan went on to tell them about the time when he told his driver in Zambia he would like to climb Mount Kilimanjaro. The driver had laughed, assuming his boss was making a joke. When Mulligan had convinced him that he was in earnest, the driver had said over his shoulder, 'But why, Mr Ambassador? When you get to the top, you will still see only Africa.' As an aside to his story, Mulligan explained that the driver had insisted on calling him 'Mr Ambassador' even though he was only a First Secretary: such elevation also enhanced the driver's status. In answer to the Zambian's question, Mulligan had been at a loss. Why climb to the top of a mountain? He managed to raise a small laugh from the others when he told them he had been tempted to hide behind that great Britishism 'because it's there, my man', but he was afraid his forefathers would, proverbially, turn in their graves.

The road was empty and Andrew Doran drove quickly in a self-assured way. Mulligan could see the army training manifesting itself. This young man, this teenage army officer who so expertly had flown them over his family farm, was back in control. The windows of the car were one-third open, the noise providing a welcome excuse for avoiding conversation. Now Mulligan watched Cahill in front, assessing what must be going through his mind. He had not seen the final farewells between brother and sister, but when Cahill came out of the house his face had lost its usual floridness and his eyes appeared to have retreated into their sockets. Mulligan was sure he had been crying. Andrew accompanied his uncle, carrying a heavy overnight bag, his arm straining.

Kennedy and Cahill dozed, the wine taking effect. Mulligan must have dozed as well when the sudden gear change, accompanied by the words 'Blast it', had them awake. As they drew close to the checkpoint blocking the road, Mulligan could see that the men were soldiers in well-worn camouflage uniforms. They were all black. Two blocked the road and a sergeant was standing confidently on the meridian line. On the hard shoulder was a large jeep with more men around it and in it. Andrew stopped so close to the two soldiers that one took a step backwards, losing the game of chicken. He rolled down his window fully and waited, staring straight ahead. The sergeant came forward and Andrew handed over his driving licence without looking at him.

Mulligan saw one of the soldiers lean over the jeep's bonnet and train his rifle on them, slowly moving the gun, taking each in his sights in turn. The rifleman lifted his head, wanting to confirm that Mulligan knew he was being monitored. Then he lowered himself behind the sights and pointed the gun at Mulligan again. No one in the car spoke. Mulligan stared into the distance, not wanting to eyeball the muzzle of a gun, but he knew it remained fixed on him. He nervously wet his lips. A muffled voice was followed by laughter from two or three men near the jeep.

The sergeant was examining the licence, but it was obvious he had long finished reading it. He placed it about a foot outside the driver's window. Andrew reached out and for one moment both men held the licence firmly, their hands almost touching, the paper tautened in their grips, their faces staring away from each other. Andrew deliberately placed the licence back on the dashboard. He rolled up the window. The sergeant focused on some point in the distance.

The two soldiers separated, moving to the sides of the road, dragging the roadblocks with them. One of them was now about a yard away from Mulligan, his face almost level as he stepped down an embankment. The soldier was small but wiry, the sinews of his arms bulging as he gripped his rifle tightly, the pockmarks on his face adding to his menace. He stepped sideways, directly into the line of sight of the muzzle on the bonnet of the jeep, deliberately blocking his comrade's view, and rubbed his jaw in the movement all men use when checking if they have shaved properly. Mulligan realised the soldier, sparing him the terror of the trained rifle, was referring to his beard. They watched each other, adjusting their heads to take account of the movement of the car. In an unmistakable movement, his big, white eyeball being covered and uncovered by the starkly contrasting dark pink eyelid, the soldier winked and smiled, the menace disappearing from his face in this silent, cryptic acknowledgement of Mulligan's beard. With the car gathering speed, Mulligan watched the soldier make the same action of rubbing his face, joking with the others who laughed at something he said.

'I think it's not just the members of the Salisbury Club who find middle-aged bearded white men remarkable,' Mulligan chuckled, and when no one answered he let his mind drift to his plans for later that evening.

Kennedy and Mulligan quickly said goodbye after Andrew had politely refused their token invitation to join them for a drink. He said goodbye formally to them, barely responding to their effusions of thanks for the visit to the farm and the trip in the plane. Andrew had made no comment on the behaviour of the officer-less soldiers or on his earlier outburst at the farm. If he was annoyed at what happened at the checkpoint, he was not going to again reveal his feelings.

'We'll let you two say goodbye in peace.' Mulligan tapped the young man's shoulder as he released his hand.

'I thought we would never get through that checkpoint alive,' Kennedy whispered to Mulligan as they entered the hotel.

'You bet. This place is kind of like watching ice cracking. The smooth surface slowly disintegrating.'

'If you don't mind, John, I'm not that hungry, so I think I'll go to my room and just get some room service later.' Kennedy had a remorseful air about him, knowing he had stepped on some very raw nerves at the farm.

Mulligan was pleased he did not have to try to get rid of him or mount some masquerade of going to his own room before returning to make contact with the night porter, on duty already. Experience had taught Mulligan to behave guilt-free. He crossed confidently over to the desk, stepping partly inside the little office where the porter had retreated as he approached.

'Good evening, sir.'

Mulligan nodded once, his face very serious, wanting to maintain his position as an esteemed hotel patron, anxious that the porter would not see him as a co-conspirator.

'Everything is arranged for nine o'clock, sir.' He waited for Mulligan to confirm his room number. Mulligan placed a Rhodesian twenty-dollar note below the counter of the desk, aware he was over-tipping.

'Thank you, sir.' The porter smiled in a polite but restrained way. Both men were mindful they should maintain a business-like approach to the deal that was being brokered. Just as Mulligan was about to leave the little office, he saw Cahill come quickly through the hotel door. Goodbyes between uncle and nephew had taken much less time than Mulligan had expected. Cahill went straight to the reception desk, cutting in front of an elderly white woman who was about to address the Jackie Kennedy look-alike. He spoke urgently to the receptionist, quickly checking left and right as he waited for his key and then rushed towards the lift. With his left arm straining, Cahill carried what Mulligan had earlier assumed was Andrew's overnight bag. Mulligan could hear Cahill's assurance on the overheard phone call. 'I promise you we'll get it sorted. That's why I'm here.' Now he grasped why Cahill had been so laid-back about his itinerary: the good senator had his own reason for visiting Rhodesia, and it was not just to pay a family visit to his older sister.

*

Mulligan sat on the edge of the bed, rubbing his damp palms on the knees of his trousers, his breath coming in shallow intakes. His erection pressed hard inside his pants. He could not believe how excited and tense he was. An image from the old black and white movies of the alcoholic trying to resist opening a whiskey bottle came to mind. For distraction, he put on the television. The news was on, being presented by a lugubrious black man who spoke in a deliberate tone. Robert Mugabe's face filled the screen, abruptly replacing footage of a plane landing at Salisbury airport, while the newsreader enthusiastically described the prime minister's trip to Moscow. The camera pulled away and Joshua Nkomo appeared, leader of the Matabele people, regarded by many as the father of Rhodesian nationalism. Mulligan watched the screen intently, his mind focusing on the main reason for their visit to Zimbabwe. Cahill must strongly mark Mugabe's cards, but could he make him understand that the future of the new African state best lay in an alliance with the West? The television news confirmed that which he had been unable to get an assurance on from any of the officials he had dealt with in preparing the itinerary. Mugabe was in Salisbury. With luck, they would get to meet him in person and not have to resort to leaving diplomatically-coded messages with one of his many minions.

The two former guerrilla leaders were deep in conversation with a great deal of smiling as Mugabe held Nkomo's elbow. The physical difference between the two men was almost comical. Mugabe was compact, seeming smaller than average next to Joshua Nkomo's huge shoulders on a frame that appeared well over six feet, his massive stomach filling his shirt to bursting point. The handsome Nkomo looked the part of the traditional African chief, in whom corpulence was a sign of strength and an important status symbol. But watching the two men in the carefully choreographed piece for the cameras, Mulligan had no doubt who was the boss. There was something about the way Nkomo tilted his head when listening to Mugabe that was too deferential from someone who was supposed to be an equal partner in the struggle for freedom. The news report went on too long, listing the dignitaries Mugabe had met in Russia and all those who turned out to meet him at the airport in Salisbury. The camera panned to what presumably were the senior civil servants who had been obliged to form a welcoming party. Mulligan laughed out loud at the obvious unease of the assembled middle-aged white men stuck in what must be their worst nightmare, and he asked himself just how much use their new friends from the Salisbury Club would be in opening the right African doors.

On the edge of the group on screen was a lone, black man who Mulligan recognised from the briefing given to him by the British diplomat. The camera was on Julius Charamba, older and more thickset than his photograph. 'Minister for Reform' in the new government, already his enemies were calling him the 'minister without a portfolio' but Charamba's self-declared mission, endorsed by Mugabe, was to watch everything that moved in the other ministries, particularly in those where the 'white influence' was seen as being too strong.

The camera was back on the newsreader again. 'Earlier today, the Irish Republican Army exchanged fire with the British army in the border area of south Armagh. The exchange lasted several minutes. No casualties were reported from either side.' Mulligan listened in a combination of amusement and fascination. This was either a cleverly constructed propaganda piece or the journalist who had taken the story from the wires did not appreciate that the Irish Republican Army was not, as the report made it sound, the army of the Irish Republic.

He jumped as the door opened.

'Ndine urombo.' The black woman spoke timidly. 'Excuse me please, mister. I knock and knock. No answer. The porter warn me not to stand in the corridor.'

*

Travelling back to Salisbury on the early Monday morning train from Bulawayo, Patricia Lynch wished she could find some excuse to return home, to cut short her now futile trip to Zimbabwe. But her responsibilities to her sponsoring aid agencies brought some sense to her thinking, and she concentrated instead on preparing a good front, particularly with Mulligan who knew her too well. Needing time to lick her very raw wounds, she hid behind the copy of the *Irish Times* that she had been deliberately carrying around with her over the past two days. On the planes and trains where she seemed to spend so much of her life as an aid co-ordinator, she used a newspaper from Ireland as a symbol of identity. In response, fellow travellers from all kinds of different backgrounds would engage her in conversation. What never ceased to amaze her was how often the most unlikely people would have some Irish connection: a priest from their schooldays, an engineer on site, or a late night singalong in some unlikely place.

Her newspaper ploy had not worked on the trip down to Bulawayo, her entry into the carriage stifling any conversation for the journey. The passengers' reception was unmistakably hostile, unlike anything she had experienced in the trains she travelled in all over Africa. She had held open the *Irish Times* so that its front title could be clearly read, trying to demonstrate that she was not a Rhodesian white woman encroaching on standard-class. It had no effect, and a sullenness filled the small compartment all the way to Bulawayo.

This morning she was using the newspaper as a screen, wanting to hide her mortification from the world, imagining that these total strangers knew what had happened. The young woman opposite, wearing a sky blue dress and matching scarf, was snoozing, mouth loosely open, the baby at her breast sucking hungrily. Her toddler daughter played with a cloth doll, covertly watching the blonde white woman. Keeping a respectful seat space distance from Patricia, a dark-suited African businessman read the previous day's *Sunday News*.

She told herself she was letting her imagination run riot, these people had no inkling of how she was feeling, but she kept her newspaper up as she looked vacantly out the window, unable to engage with the words on the page. The issues in Ireland of the previous Friday seemed so far away. It was something she always experienced in Africa: a sense of breaking connections, of entering a different world, a different time. She watched the city of Bulawayo falling into perspective, surrounded by hills of granite jagging into the blue sky.

The main cause of her lack of concentration was the empty ache in her stomach. She was behaving like a lovesick teenager and was in turn angry with herself, caught in a maelstrom of self-pity and self-anger. What had she hoped to achieve by this journey? Normal people do not put their lives on hold for more than ten years without hearing from their lovers and assume they will meet again and carry on as before. Not in the real world anyway. These were the questions she should have put to herself in Ireland. Long ago. Knowing this made her feel even more stupid. And angry. At best she had been stupid, or was it blind, to imagine he was waiting for her. So blind that what she found out had never even crossed her mind.

Yesterday morning seemed like a lifetime away. She had woken early, her simple plan already worked out. Her basic research from the evening before had given her the same information that she had established from Ireland two days before she heard about the trip to Rhodesia. Every six months she had rung the hospital in Bulawayo and asked for her lover. The answers were usually brusque, telling her they had no doctor of that name. The first time she had drawn a blank she assumed that he had joined the guerrillas in the bush and that this had been his intention all along. She would wait. The war could not last forever. Everyone said UDI had to end soon.

For months she thought about him every day, many times, no matter how busy she was. She prayed he was alive, nothing more, suspending her deepest wishes for them both, together again in some undefined, blissful place, afraid to even think about what he could be going through if he had chosen to go to war. In the emergency aid work where she was investing her energy, she was seeing enough of the aftermath of African conflicts to know how callous death could be on a continent where life appeared cheap at the best of times. But as the fighting in Rhodesia dragged on year after year, she phoned and phoned, a sign of her faithfulness, each time listening to the same brusque negatives. She waited until the elections were over, until she could be sure that the hostilities had finally ended, and rang the hospital in Bulawayo again. The receptionist paused when she heard the name. Patricia could not breathe.

'No.'

She felt her chest tighten, her mouth going dry. Why had she expected this phone call would be any different to the others?

'He is not here. He is away.'

He is away! He is alive! Maybe he had forgotten about her but at least he was alive! Could she tell her where he had gone? Get a message to him? When would he be back from his travels? No, she could not tell her that. The receptionist refused to tell her any more and hung up. Patricia listened to the burr of the broken connection, a tenuous link of sound to him. She was not aware that she was crying. There were no sobs or heaves, just a trickle of tears. Of joy! Of relief! She gathered her things and walked to the diving board, stepping off into the cold sea, sinking down, down, feeling the pressure on her chest. Rising, up, up, up, breaking the surface with a whoop of joy.

Had he finally done what he said he would do and joined the staff at Bulawayo hospital? Surely he would be a welcome addition to offset the haemorrhage of white doctors unwilling to live under the new regime? Or had he been there all along, hidden from her questioning by unhelpful white receptionists? This was the puzzle Patricia presented to herself as she sat in the taxi taking her from the grandly wide main streets of the town centre into the suburbs. Due to the hospital's obdurate unhelpfulness or genuine regard for his privacy, she had arrived in Bulawayo without an address, yet filled with certainty that she could find him. She had a plan.

The name meant nothing to the first taxi driver but he insisted on helping. How many black doctors are there in Bulawayo she was asking herself in exasperation, watching him consult with the rest of the drivers hanging around outside the hotel. Suddenly, one of them broke away and came lolloping towards her, rubbing his hands, gloating with the advantage he had over the others. Yes, he knew where the doctor lived, please come with him.

The taxi stopped outside a closed, high gate to a garden surrounded by an equally tall, well-trimmed privet hedge, creating a natural stockade around the house. On the left pillar was a small wrought iron sign with the words 'The Downs' inscribed in white through a motif of red roses. She let the taxi go and walked away from the house through the leafy suburbia. Her lover had done well. Or was this house one of the spoils of war? For about an hour she wandered around the Sunday morning streets. There were a few other pedestrians and less cars, but no one paid any heed to her. She told herself that he might, he must, be married. Why else would he be living in the big house that surely hid beyond the secrecy of the hedge and the high gate? But at least he was alive. Now she could talk to him again. After that, one never knew what might happen. She pulled a rope hanging over the gate and a bell sounded deep inside the garden. She waited, fighting the temptation to slip away. Just when she was about to lose her nerve, the gate was partly opened. A young black man dressed like a soldier barred her way. The cover of his holster was undone and she could clearly see the butt of his pistol. He waited for her to speak, giving her no acknowledgement.

'Is the doctor at home?'

The young man considered her. His self-assurance was unnerving. 'Are you a patient?'

'No. I mean, yes.'

He warily made his assessment. 'The doctor, he is not here.'

'I am an old friend of the doctor and I have come a very long way to see him. I come from Ireland. You know where Ireland is?'

The guard considered her impassively. He closed the gate until it was just wide enough for her to be able to see his face.

'I knew the doctor when he was in Biafra, in Nigeria, many years ago.'

An inch of a gap remained. She placed her foot at the base of the gate so that it could move no further, not caring what the consequences might be from this menacing young man. 'Please, please, it's very important. Just go tell the doctor Patricia is here.'

She heard a woman's voice in what sounded like a North American accent. The gate swung open and Patricia found herself facing a blonde white woman of about her own age. How long had she been there? How much had she heard?

'Can I help you?' The woman spoke formally, a hint of suspicion in her voice. She was wearing a three-quarter length white bathrobe and her short hair was wet, sleeked back from her face, fresh from a shower or a swimming pool.

'I was hoping to…to… is the doctor at home?'

'He is away.' For additional emphasis, perhaps to let Patricia know of their status, she added, 'On official business.'

The two women faced each other, both at a loss as to what to do next. The guard had stepped behind the gate, leaving the two of them alone under the morning sun, holding their ground. Patricia was about to ask where had the doctor gone when a boy's voice called, 'Hey, mom, what's up?'

The familiar face appearing at the woman's shoulder startled her. Despite the lighter colour from the mixed parentage, it was recognizable, so very, very recognizable. Her lover's almost teenage son was standing beside his mother. Patricia went to step forward, wanting to touch him, but retreated from what she was seeing, her hand moving outwards, her body backwards. Unable to speak, she scrutinised the boy, fascinated by the embodiment of her lover's deceit, repulsed by the realisation of what she was finding out. The boy eyed her nervously, not understanding why his arrival should have such an effect on this stranger. His mother followed her son's look back to Patricia. She moved in front of him, wanting to protect him. Her voice was cold.

'You must forgive our son.' She let the emphasis on the

ownership of the handsome boy imprint itself on the understanding the two women were sharing. 'He is still adjusting from his forward Canadian ways.'

Remembering this scene as the train moved through the dry, brown landscape, Patricia cringed. Somehow she had moved away from the gate without completely losing control. Then she walked and walked, not caring what direction she was taking, not noticing the dreariness of the small apartment blocks and little rows of dilapidated houses trying to hide behind the unkempt bushes and straggly clothes lines. The two policemen were very polite, even deferential towards the bewildered white woman. Was she lost? Does she not know this is not a safe part of town for her to be in? Could they help her? She was a long way from her hotel. They would have to insist on bringing her there. She went straight to her room, locking the door to shut out her humiliation. She did not cry, but wanted to. She did nothing except sit and follow the time passing in the changing light coming through the blinds, the brightness giving way to a gentle glow, changing to a gloomy shadow that was soon dark.

Mulligan and Kennedy walked slowly along the empty footpath, wanting to use up the fifteen minutes they had to spare before their ten o'clock appointment. The branches of the Jacaranda trees brought them through slivers of light and shadow under the clear blue skies.

'With the local dollar almost on a par with us it's easy to get a handle on these prices. But I'm not a great shopper, Tom, so am I right in thinking that the high-quality goods are dearer than home?'

'Maybe we should consult our esteemed senator. Mr Conspicuous Consumption.'

'Yeah. I'm sure he'd know the price of a pint of milk.'

'Somehow I don't think so, John. We won't give him that much credit. But I'm sure he could tell us the cost of a pair of French knickers.'

Mulligan was amused at the acidity in the younger man's voice and Kennedy was obviously enjoying the shared disloyalty towards their absent boss.

'I really wish I had the spunk to ring him this morning, just to disturb his lie-in, and pretend I was checking if he had changed his mind about coming to this meeting.' Kennedy sounded wistful.

"I can just imagine.' Mulligan added, in a poor imitation of Cahill's growl, 'Get me a fucking meeting with Mugabe!'

'A meeting with Mugabe? That sounds like my cue, Tom.' At that a white suited black man with an open neck white shirt fell in beside them. Kennedy blushed at the over-familiarity of the American.

'You must be the "man from Nairobi".' Mulligan extended his hand, in control of the situation.

Jack Clay laughed. 'I see Tom has been keeping you posted.'

'You'd be surprised,' Mulligan replied, cryptically. 'Isn't that right, Tom?' Then he added, smiling broadly at the American. 'I hope you're not spying on us now, are you?'

'Don't you worry, John,' the American laughed again as he used Mulligan's name before being introduced, 'we don't spy on our friends.'

At that, he patted Kennedy on the elbow as he stepped around him. 'See you guys later maybe.'

Kennedy glanced over his shoulder, nervously checking that the American had really gone. 'How the blazes did you know who he was?'

'Just a hunch.' Mulligan was teasing the younger man and did not feel it necessary to tell him the detail of the US ambassador's briefing in Dublin.

'And he knew your name as well!' Kennedy wanted Mulligan to know he did not want to be taken for a ride.

'I think you'll find, Tom, that most of Zimbabwe's early visitors have an agenda. Next time you're in the dining room, have a good dekko. The KGB are even easier to spot than the CIA. And poor diplomats like Jack Clay and ourselves spend our time trying not to get confused with the real spooks. We are all the "early birds trying to catch a worm", and do not repeat that analogy before we touch down in Dublin. I don't think the supporters of Comrades Mugabe and Nkomo would be too pleased.'

Towering in front of them was the tallest building they had seen in Salisbury, the thirteen storeys home to four Government ministries. The foyer seemed dark as they stepped out of the glare. Just inside the shadows, a one-legged black man was selling newspapers, the empty length of his long pants floating gently in the breeze created by the open door. The uniformed security man vetted their details and rang upstairs. They waited at the desk, casually checking out their surroundings.

On Mulligan's assignment to Zambia many years before he had been struck by the similarity between the reception areas of the government offices he visited and the foyers of many of the government departments in Dublin. Usually there were five or six men just hanging around, some of them porters waiting to run errands, but there always appeared to be one or two who were surplus to requirements, the result of high unemployment whereby there were lots of men happy to kill time. And a caller usually had to wait what seemed like a long time before one of them would volunteer assistance, finally distinguishing between the under-employed and the unemployed. But this Salisbury reception area was unlike any other African foyer he had been in, with its air of unflustered, English efficiency. It was, Mulligan felt, yet another of the many small reminders that Rhodesia was a country in Africa run by Europeans.

'Gentlemen, I will bring you to Mr Thompson's office.' The middle-aged black man in a white shirt with blue tie did not introduce himself. They hurried after him wordlessly. He opened the door of the office and stood back to let them enter.

'Ah, the chappies from Éire.'

They must have walked into Biggles's office was Mulligan's first thought, taken aback at the sight of the plump, ruddy-faced

Englishman, with what must surely be a waxed moustache? The short-sleeved shirt, knee length khaki pants, socks stopping below the knees, rooted in glistening black shoes, all adding to the effect.

'I'm Thompson, Deputy Secretary. The Secretary has been called away and he asked me to see you.' He extended big handshakes, requesting them to sit at the table.

'William, will you organise some tea like a good chap.'

Mulligan thanked Thompson, outlining how difficult it had been to get appointments by phone from Ireland and how appreciative they were that the Deputy Secretary was available to meet them at such short notice. He cautiously explained the purpose of their visit, the desire of the Irish government and EEC to open diplomatic relations with the former guerrillas, gauging Thompson's reaction to see if he was offended by their efforts to bypass the current administration. Thompson sighed, indicating that he was not surprised with their agenda, encouraging Mulligan to reveal the core of their intent.

'Are we naïve in hoping to get to meet Mugabe?'

'I'm afraid I can't help you in that quarter, old boy.' He spoke matter-of-factly and then gave a small laugh. 'My colour isn't Comrade Mugabe's favourite just now. Isn't that right, William?'

The black man raised his head from his tea pouring, but did not reply. The unanswered question hung between the two. Thompson lifted an ornate wooden letter opener, pressing the ends between his index fingers, a tiny tremor the only indicator of his feelings.

'We had a very interesting visit to Eamonn Doran's farm yesterday.' Mulligan was searching for a way of connecting with this Englishman, reckoning that the Rhodesian white community were even more tightly knit than usual in colonial Africa.

'Eddie Doran, don't tell me you know Eddie!' Thompson leant back, at ease. He now knew which side they were on. 'Eddie and I play poker once a month. Just for cents mind you, I wouldn't have the dosh of chappies like him.' His face went serious. 'Terrible about his young lad. Terrible, terrible business.' There were mumbles of sympathy all round.

'Men like Eddie have made Rhodesia what it is. They don't call it "the bread basket of Africa" for nothing, you know.' Thompson walked to the window. 'It's all gone now.' He spoke across the urban skyline towards the horizon. 'We have reached the beginning of the Marxist end. You mark my words. The farms of Rhodesia will run with blood.' Mulligan thought he saw his shoulders droop.

'We have always treated the black people very well. They're the best off in Africa. We have no famines here.' He faced them. 'Isn't that right, William?'

The black man had been in the room all the time, waiting for his next instruction. After a small cough he replied. 'Excuse me, Deputy Secretary. I did not catch what you said.'

Thompson came back to his desk and sat down again. 'A few hotheads with support from the commies have managed to take it all away.'

Mulligan and Kennedy were at a loss as to what to say, conscious of the silent scrutiny of Thompson's assistant. 'I'm sure you've all come through difficult times,' Mulligan ventured.

'The reason, Mr Mulligan, that you're finding it so hard to get appointments is that we do not know whether we are coming or going.' Thompson snorted at the little pun he had stumbled on. 'But I think you can take it that we're going. Mostly to South Africa, although it won't be long before it goes down the tubes as well.' He turned away from them again. 'Lizzie would like us to return to England, but I cannot see what a middle-aged ex senior civil servant can do in Thatcher's England.'

'What about your pension?'

Mulligan almost jumped on Kennedy. Was asking stupid questions his role in life? Thompson snorted again. 'Young man, you hardly expect these Marxist traitors to have that kind of honour. We will leave here with little more than the shirts on our backs and empty promises. Everything will be lost, all lost.'

'That's just awful. I'm really sorry. I shouldn't have asked.'

'Will you listen to me,' Thompson was obviously jollying himself into action, 'I'm cribbing like an old woman. I can pick up the phone to Corbett over in Finance or Hamilton in Industry and get you meetings. But they are in the same boat as myself. They have no line to Mugabe.' He picked up the file on his desk and strongly grasped the Irishmen's hands as if compensating for the futility of the meeting. The assistant held the door for them and followed them towards the lift. All three got in. William pressed the control panel and spoke towards the closing doors. 'I have worked with Mr Thompson for six years. He is a fair man, but does not understand. He has never understood. Three per cent of the people cannot use the country for their own benefit.' He let this information sink in. 'I will arrange for you to meet Minister Charamba. I think he can get you to Comrade Mugabe.'

Mulligan and Kennedy stepped out, saying effusive goodbyes to William, who impassively waited for the doors to close again.

Patricia Lynch joined them just as they were about to order lunch. With a quick group hello, she studied the menu. Mulligan continued briefing Cahill on the morning's meeting, insisting he was not exaggerating Thompson's colonial Englishness. She could see Mulligan had an ace up his sleeve, that he was deliberately exaggerating the fruitlessness of the meeting. When he came to describe the message delivered in the lift, Mulligan graciously handed the story over to Kennedy. 'There we were, coming away empty-handed, when the most amazing thing happened. Isn't that right, Tom.' Kennedy took the prompt and continued, trying to inflect Mulligan's drama into the story. Despite his morning at the rooftop pool, Cahill was not in much of a mood for stories.

'So where the hell does that leave us?' Cahill impatiently ended any suspense. Mulligan lifted the water jug and filled his glass.

'More water, Senator?'

Cahill dismissed the offer with a sharp movement of his hand.

'It leaves us...Senator...' Mulligan deliberately filled Patricia's glass. '...it leaves us with an appointment to see Julius Charamba, all-knowing and all-seeing Minister for Reform at three o'clock this afternoon.' Before Kennedy could ask, Mulligan added, 'I got a phone call just before lunch.'

Mulligan then turned to Patricia Lynch. 'And tell us, Patricia, how are they all down in Bulawayo?'

'They certainly don't appear as organised as up here.' She was bluffing, trading off her superficial impressions. Mulligan raised an interrogative eyebrow, but Patricia's napkin suddenly required careful unfolding.

'Will this Charamba character get us to Mugabe?' Cahill did not bother to conceal his annoyance at Mulligan for stringing him along. Mulligan tilted back his head and pointed his bearded chin at Cahill.

'We'll just have to wait and see. Won't we? Senator.'

Part of Tom Kennedy wished Mulligan would stop winding up Cahill as he was going to suffer the brunt of the senator's wrath in turn, but he admired his senior colleague's blasé attitude.

They were met in the ministry's reception area by a young white man dressed in a cream suit, his red tie contrasting with the whiteness of his wide shirt collar. He was deeply tanned and his blonde hair was parted in the middle. He did not introduce himself, just approached the Irish team as their eyes were adjusting from the brightness of the street. 'Please come with me.' His English, public school accent summoned them. Opening the door to the stairwell, he thumbed towards the lift and said disdainfully, 'I'm afraid their lifts are out of order,' leaving no doubt that this failure had anything to do with him.

From the back of the single file line making their way up the stairs, Mulligan said, 'These things happen.'

The young man opened the door and held it as they moved into the corridor. When Mulligan drew abreast with him, he said, 'Perhaps.'

They had already entered the outer office, with three of the desks occupied by middle-aged white men, when he added, 'Or maybe it's just a sign of things to come.' He moved quickly to the front of the group, opened another door and stiffly ushered them through. He did not follow.

Standing at the opposite side of a small, plain beech table were three black men. Mulligan recognised Julius Charamba and deliberately called him 'Minister' as formal handshakes were exchanged across the table, full names given without titles. Charamba flickered at the recognition and then, not to be outdone, he said 'Senator' to Cahill, gesturing them to be seated. There was room for only three chairs on each side of the table. Cahill and Charamba sat in the centre, flanked by their teams. Kennedy pulled over an extra chair, took up position next to Mulligan and opened his folder in a display of seriousness, feeling conspicuous at the head of the table.

Mid-way through Cahill's introductory remarks, Minister Julius Charamba leant to one of his colleagues, talking rapidly in chiShona. Cahill pulled himself up and glowerred at Kennedy, eager to blame somebody for this rudeness. The Irish delegation watched as a lengthy exchange ensued, speckled with laughter, evidently calculated to put the visitors in their place. Mulligan leant towards Kennedy so that the Africans did not see him wink. 'I hope those boyos aren't laughing at our expense,' he said in Irish.

He watched Kennedy's mouth fall open, but knew from the young man's worried glance towards the Africans that at least he understood.

'They can laugh at our esteemed senator all they want, but the permanent government deserves more respect.' Remembering the note from the American official, 'Springboks 15, Irish Anti-Apartheid movement 6,000', Mulligan added, 'I've got a feeling someone has brought extra baggage into the room.' Mulligan was taking sinful pleasure at Kennedy's panic on hearing his boss being spoken of so cynically, secure in the knowledge that Cahill did not understand a word. Perhaps he recognised 'seanadóir', for senator, as Cahill's annoyance appeared to be rocketing. He poked Mulligan sharply in the ribs, wanting to roar, 'Is everyone in the room going to talk around me in other bloody languages?'

'Wait and see, our cúpla focal will put some manners on our African friends.' Mulligan ignored Cahill as he tried to get Kennedy to engage in his charade. 'But, in the name of God, will you say something so that we can at least let on we're having some kind of conversation.' Mulligan spoke emphatically at Kennedy, forcing a response. Kennedy gulped and took a deep breath, the colour draining from his cheeks.

'Ár nAthair, atá ar neamh...'Mulligan watched incredulously. '...go naofar tAinm...' Kennedy, his panic at being asked to engage in the pretence throttling his inventiveness, was reciting the Lord's Prayer, '... go dtaga do ríocht...'.

Charamba stopped speaking, head to one side, listening like a bird. We're having the desired effect at least, Mulligan thought, nodding at Kennedy, urging him to continue.

'...go ndeantar do thoil ar an dtalamh'

'Seanadóir,' Charamba called out, 'how thrilled I am to hear your native tongue again after all these years.' He spoke slowly, his African inflection stilting his near-perfect Irish, directly at Cahill, knowing he did not understand, smiling broadly at him. Cahill remained stone-faced. It was Mulligan's turn to gulp. Patricia Lynch giggled. Tom Kennedy continued half-heartedly, his voice trailing off in the acceptance that this really was not a good idea.

'I'm sure the Senator is fascinated to hear his native tongue spoken so fluently far away from home.' Mulligan spoke on behalf of Cahill, in Irish, trying to get Charamba's attention, but the African kept Cahill in his sights, intent on using his advantage.

'If not also a little surprised to see what the gorillas have been learning all this time.' Charamba continued in Irish but used the English word 'gorilla', mispronouncing 'guerrilla' so that Cahill would have no doubt the direction this conversation was taking, driving home his point. Cahill moved, about to get up. He was recovering his composure, about to assert himself by storming out of the room.

'Ah, Senator Cahill, how delightful to have an opportunity to use my rusty Irish.' Speaking English again, Charamba's earlier slight American accent appeared to have broadened. Cahill eased himself back into the chair. 'I have always been an admirer of the Irish colonial struggle. Ever since my days at Trinity College, on the first UN scholarship I was offered during UDI, I have had a great regard for your country. I spent many weeks in Connemara with a lovely fellow student who I believe is now making her reputation as a vocal member of your Labour Party. Why, you may even have in her the makings of your first female Taoiseach.'

'What a surprise, Minister Charamba, to meet an Hibernophile.' Cahill's voice was flat and he caustically added, 'A surprise indeed, Mr. Mulligan!'

'And, Senator Cahill, may I add before you have Comrade Mulligan's "guts for garters" as my Irish cailín was so fond of saying, the reason TCD does not appear on my lengthy, with due thanks to the munificence of the United Nations, CV is that regrettably I never took my degree. I had a disagreement with the functionaries of your State over, shall we say, a public order issue concerning a certain rugby team.' Charamba was enjoying himself, fully in control of the meeting. Before his visitors could recover their composure, he pushed back his chair and rose, his colleagues following suit. 'But gentleman, and comrade lady, forgive me, I am under pressure to be elsewhere. Let us defer business for now and let me invite you to a barbecue this evening so that we can share with you some real Zimbabwean hospitality.'

He raised his hands, palms facing them, the pink in contrast to the gleam of his black face: they were dismissed. No real business had been dealt with; they had hardly got past the opening introductions. Mulligan could see that Charamba had agreed to meet them just as part of some game. If so, what was it about? Cahill jumped to his feet and moved around his chair, holding its back, increasing the distance between him and Charamba. Mulligan could see Cahill's knuckles whiten as he tightened his grip and for a moment he thought the chair might break. The senator spoke through his bared teeth. 'I'm sure Mr Mulligan would be delighted to accept.' Cahill left, without extending his hand or waiting to see if Charamba would extend his. Mulligan had to admire him. Cahill was not known as a street-fighter politician for nothing. In diplomatic terms he had just told Charamba to go stuff himself, while leaving the door partially open for further negotiations.

The tension left the room with Cahill and the Zimbabweans came around the table, warmly saying goodbye to the rest of the Irish delegation. Charamba even jokingly kissed Patricia's hand, to the open amusement of his African comrades. As Mulligan said goodbye to Charamba, he tightened his grip and said in Irish, 'Thank you, Minister.'

'Mr Mulligan, my name is Morgan Nkomo. Minister Charamba asked me to collect you.' Mulligan noticed the hesitancy he placed on the word 'Minister', almost finding it difficult to say. The big man extended his hand. With his broad face sitting on a massive pair of shoulders, Morgan Nkomo bore a small resemblance to his namesake, Joshua Nkomo, the leader of the Matabele people. Unlike his namesake, however, Morgan Nkomo's chest was bigger than his stomach, flat as a board in the tight-fitting Mao Tse Tung uniform. Here was a man who would have no problem passing an army physical fitness test, Mulligan thought as Nkomo's right hand enveloped his, then opened in a half rotation and closed again, before releasing slowly. A handshake, African style. The first since he arrived two days ago.

Outside Meikles Hotel a black Mercedes in showroom condition gleamed in the late afternoon sun. Although never very good on car models, Mulligan knew it was almost twenty years old: no new vehicles had been available for importation during UDI. Nkomo opened the driver's door and Mulligan moved quickly around to the front passenger side. If this was some kind of test, he wanted to err on the side of caution. Years earlier in Zambia his driver had convinced him not to sit in the front and to take his place in the back like all the other embassy officials. 'People will not understand how important you are, Ambassador Mulligan, if you sit beside me,' his Zambian driver had earnestly explained. It was the second part of his argument that was the clincher. 'If they do not understand how important you are, then people will not respect me as your driver.' So he had sat in the back and let the car door be opened for him, making his contribution to the maintenance of social order. But it was clear to him that Morgan Nkomo was no ordinary driver. The familiarity of his handshake, his open directness said that this man had never been a servant to anyone.

'I hope you are having an interesting time in Rhode...Zimbabwe?'

'Yes. It's my very first time.'

Nkomo realised the emphasis and laughed, 'I'm glad to hear you weren't sneaking in and out during UDI, breaking the so-called "embargo".'

'Well, at the risk of sounding cynical, it was easy for us to observe the embargo as Ireland didn't have much trade with Rhodesia before UDI, so I'm not going to bullshit you with platitudes about our position.'

'But it's not your first visit to Africa.'

'No. I learned the African handshake during a spell of duty in Lusaka.'

The big man burst into laughter again. 'The "African handshake". Indeed, Mister Mulligan. We like to think of it as the "African acid test". It is how we check out who really sees us as equals. Who can really be our friends. Sometimes I go very "African" with our English visitors, and their limp handshakes, and I refuse to let go. Keep a nice, warm grip.'

'Well, Morgan, it's one way of making the Brits feel at home.' Mulligan knew he was taking a chance, using the first name so soon.

'But John, we have so much to learn from you Irish about making the Brits feel at home.' They both laughed now, comfortably: their equal status confirmed.

'An interesting city. In part so colonial that it doesn't seem African at all,' Nkomo said, reading Mulligan's thoughts as they were leaving the well-ordered streets of central Salisbury.

'A little bit of England,' Mulligan added, as they passed the well-tended lawns and neat hedges.

'Each patch of England is a credit to underpaid African gardeners and under-worked colonial housewives. I'm taking you by the scenic route. Over there is the suburb of Harare, the real African part of Salisbury. Maybe later we will see the shantytowns. A problem that has increased sharply with the influx of displaced people from the countryside during the war of liberation.'

The party was in full swing when they arrived. Nkomo introduced him to various people, all black, shepherding him through the scattered groupings. The handshakes were formal, with none of Nkomo's warmth or what Mulligan had been used to in his days in Zambia. At the far end of the garden, Charamba was talking earnestly to the only other white person present.

'I believe you've met Julius Charamba already.'

Mulligan took his cue and said 'Hello Julius', carefully monitoring Charamba to ensure the dropping of his ministerial designation was not causing offence. Charamba did not appear to notice any familiarity. Was he naturally informal, or was the non-use of his title a studied part of an adopted Marxist outlook? On the other hand, as Mulligan well knew, having seen a series of politicians come and go as ministers, the informality might just be the result of Charamba not yet being used to his new-found moniker. The man with Charamba stepped forward.

'Welcome to Rhode...Zimbabwe. I'm Patrick Moriarty, I work with Julius in the Ministry.' Shaking Mulligan's hand, he added, 'Sorry for not returning your calls but Julius wanted to play it this way. I would have loved to have been at today's meeting to see Cahill fall into our little mantrap.'

They all laughed, and Mulligan realised he was being brought into their conspiracy.

'Mr John Mulligan,' Charamba spoke in a tone of earnest disbelief, 'the Western world does not realise the obvious. Rhodesia and the people in it, particularly the white community, have been cut off for the past fifteen years, but the people of Zimbabwe were not. Most of us here in this garden have only just returned home. We have been working in government departments in the USA, Canada, England. We have studied at the leading universities in the English-speaking world, including Trinity…' He laughed and bowed slightly towards the two Irishmen, '… your own venerable institution.'

'Yes, I'm realising things are not quite what they seem,' Mulligan smiled too broadly, not wanting to appear churlish on Cahill's behalf.

'We have also had available to us some of the best intelligence services in the world.' Mulligan guessed that this was a reference to the KGB. 'We know your Senator Cahill's track record on black and white issues only too well. Indeed, I have had some personal exposure to it. Maybe after this little visit he might think twice about leading demonstrations in favour of racist rugby tours. Or supporting your chain stores who insist on not observing embargos. Remember John, Zimbabwe is not Zambia.'

Charamba paused, ensuring that Mulligan had got the message. Cahill was not the only one they had checked out.

'When Zambia gained independence in 1964, it had available to it about seventy native Zambians with third level degrees. Why, we have more graduates at this little soirée, most of them with doctorates and work experience.' Charamba surveyed the guests at the garden party, calculating the weight of their education. 'Zimbabwe will be the jewel in the crown of Africa, of black, free Africa.' He had addressed himself to both white men, appearing to want to drive home a point with Moriarty as well. Nkomo remained detached.

'I'm afraid I'm one of those white men who has been cut off,' Patrick Moriarty said. 'I haven't been ho…back to Ireland in more than thirty years.'

'A lot has changed since then.' Mulligan directed his conversation from Charamba to Moriarty, unsure of his ground on Rhodesian-Zimbabwean affairs. They chatted about Ireland. Inevitably the North became the focus of conversation. Nkomo and Charamba were incisive with their questioning, unwilling to go along with Mulligan's diplomatic manoeuvring around issues they saw in much simpler terms. Eventually, Nkomo said in an exasperated tone, 'John, John, the English are occupying part of your country. You have an army, why don't you use it?'

Before Mulligan could reply there was a hush across the volume of the polite chit-chat. People were moving a few steps, clearing a path, all turning to face the same way. A compact man in a short-sleeved shirt and razor-creased long pants was moving through the crowd, stopping to talk to small groups in intense bursts. No one dared approach him. Mulligan observed the display of power from Robert Mugabe, the former guerrilla leader who had been the target of the odium of the Western media. This was the man they had come to woo on behalf of the EEC: the man whose Marxist beliefs could lead southern Africa to communism. When Mugabe had arrived, Mulligan thought he was unaccompanied, but now he could see the four bodyguards, about ten feet apart, moving in unison with the new premier like panthers. Despite the heat, they were the only ones wearing jackets, no doubt to hide their armoury. In an obvious display of status, Charamba stepped towards Mugabe.

'Let me welcome you home properly, Comrade Robert,' he laughed as they embraced. He brought Mugabe towards them, ignoring Nkomo and Moriarty. 'This is Mr Mulligan, the senior civil servant from the Irish delegation.'

Mugabe extended his hand. Mulligan decided to say the minimum, sticking to, 'I'm very honoured to meet you,' fairly sure Mugabe would not believe any congratulations offered. Mugabe did not reply to the greeting. He limply held Mulligan's hand. 'I understand your senator wishes to meet me.' His tone was cool, aloof. 'Julius will make the arrangements.'

Mugabe was about to advance, the audience over, when he

added, 'My indebtedness to your Bishop Donal Lamont means that I can just about forgive the Irish delegation in its choice of mission leaders.' He spoke disdainfully, his eyes narrowing behind his wide-framed, heavy glasses. 'And in your choice of dining companions.' He moved away, not bothering to wait for Mulligan's reaction.

'You won't go rushing back to the Salisbury Club after that slap on the wrist,' Moriarty whispered as soon as Mugabe bestowed his attention on another group. Squeezing Mulligan's elbow gently, he said more loudly, 'C'mon over here and meet my wife and sons.' When they had moved out of earshot of the Africans, Moriarty started chuckling. 'I'm really sorry I missed Charamba slagging off Cahill. Young Julius has been plotting something ever since he intercepted your telex to me.'

Mulligan furrowed his brow, wanting to impress on him that he was not sure what was going on. Moriarty stopped and moved closer to Mulligan. 'When Charamba was arrested for a breach of the peace for his part in the anti-Springboks' demonstration, the Irish government withdrew its co-funding of the UN scholarship.'

Mulligan tut-tutted in mock horror, acknowledging the significance of what he was hearing.

'He had to leave Trinity and finish his degree in the States. Yale, no less.'

'Poor divil.' Mulligan spoke under his breath, feigning sympathy. They both laughed, but then Moriarty's face became very serious.

'I don't want to know why you're here, John. I'm not going to break a lifetime policy of keeping my head down. Not now, when I can't be sure just who might want to decapitate me. But let me tell you, Cahill is the wrong man in the wrong place. Mugabe might give him two minutes out of a genuine feeling of respect for Bishop Lamont. But believe you me, I don't think Cahill has a snowball's chance of making any headway with Mugabe. And his real motives for being here are under suspicion.'

Before Mulligan could question him, Moriarty said, 'John, I'd like you to meet my better half, Daya, and my sons, Banga and Patrick.'

*

Morgan Nkomo drove through the streets, empty but for the unnervingly frequent open-backed army lorries full of black soldiers with guns resting on their knees. Despite their ominous presence, Mulligan was in an expansive mood. With a meeting in place with Mugabe for Wednesday, and another of his "little arrangements" fixed up for tonight, everything really was falling into place. Nkomo was not being very responsive, and Mulligan thought it strange that he parked in a car space and did not just double-park in front of the hotel to drop him off. As he opened the door, Nkomo firmly laid a hand on his forearm. 'I must meet with your senator.' He tightened his grip to underline the urgency in his voice.

'I'm sure he would be delighted to meet you, Morgan. We have a fairly open schedule tomorrow, so why don't you join us for lunch.'

'No, I think it would be better if we met now in more private circumstances.' At that, Nkomo quickly got out of the car and came around to Mulligan's side.

'OK Morgan, but let me warn you, Cahill can be cantankerous.'

Never a dull moment, Mulligan said to himself, leading the way into the hotel. Cahill and Kennedy were in the dining room where a small orchestra of about ten black men in morning suits was playing to the mostly empty chairs. Patricia Lynch was nowhere to be seen, and there were only two settings at the table. Mulligan made the introductions, giving Nkomo undue credit for getting the meeting with Mugabe. Cahill was gracious, insisting on filling him a freshly ordered wine glass. Nkomo was the only black customer, but he did not seem to notice the glances from the other tables. The pleasantries were barely exhausted when Nkomo said firmly, 'I need to talk to the senator in private.'

Kennedy jumped, not even waiting for his dismissal to be confirmed by Cahill. Mulligan shifted uncomfortably. Was he going to be dismissed as well by his evening's companion? But Nkomo fixed directly on Cahill as soon as Kennedy left the table. 'I think, Senator, it would be better if we did our business in your penthouse suite.'

Not for the first time did Mulligan admire the way information was very pointedly given away by their Zimbabwean hosts, wanting it to be recognised just how much they knew about their visitors. Nkomo led the way to the lift. Mulligan ignored Cahill's annoyance, and the three men did not speak again until they were in the penthouse suite, Mulligan and Cahill on the two armchairs, creating an audience for Nkomo who occupied the sofa across from them. 'Firstly, John, to answer the question you were too polite to ask me earlier. Am I related to Joshua Nkomo? Yes. His father and mine are from the same village.' He waited for them to digest this information, and added, 'We have worked together for many years.'

Mulligan laughed quietly at the euphemism, but Cahill watched silently, alert, his guard up against this big man who had so successfully taken control of his evening.

'As you will know, Senator, the colony of Rhodesia occupies the land of two main tribes: Bulawayo, 250 miles from here is the capital of Matabeleland, while you are currently in the capital of the Shona people. My people, the Matabele, through our leader, Joshua Nkomo, have...have co-operated with ZANU, which is largely a Shona party, and Mugabe to reach a settlement with the white occupiers of our country that is acceptable to the British. We are now moving into the next stage of our struggle for liberation and equality.' Nkomo clapped his hands. 'I'm sure, of course, you know all this and that Mr Mulligan has been assiduous in his preparation of your briefing material.' There seemed to be a touch of sarcasm in his voice. Cahill stifled a yawn.

'We know why you are here, Senator, and we know Mugabe is flattered to be wooed by the West. Despite his Marxist mouthings, he knows that greater economic advantage will flow from maintaining links with the West and he will be keen to find a way of keeping doors open without seeming too receptive to the Brits.'

'I'm very interested to hear that,' Cahill said coldly. 'And I look forward to meeting Prime Minister Mugabe,' he added, standing up, signalling the end of the meeting. Nkomo remained seated. 'Senator, we have a crisis on our hands in Matabeleland. Our army bore the brunt of the war with Ian Smith. Many of our most seasoned soldiers are still in the bush and there is great disarray. We know Mugabe has no intention of sharing power with Joshua Nkomo and the Matabele people. He is going to move against us and I fear we will suffer many casualties.'

Mulligan watched Cahill steel himself.

'Mr Nkomo, as you can appreciate, I cannot comment on what you have just speculated...'

'Senator, when my "speculation" proves to be correct, my people will be destroyed.' Nkomo sprang out of his chair and moved towards Cahill, the menace in his voice making it clear that he was demanding, not asking. 'The message you will deliver to Mugabe is that the Western powers are aware of his intentions: that you will collectively act to prevent any purge against us, the Matabele people. I...we believe that if it is clearly communicated to Mugabe that his intentions are known, then he will re-think his strategy. You will also tell him how much the West values the contribution from Mr Joshua Nkomo and that you would find it very difficult to build bridges with Zimbabwe without his presence in the international arena into the future.'

Cahill stood facing Nkomo. Mulligan watched the two men. If this were to be hand-to-hand combat, he would not fancy Cahill's chances against the towering and now very agitated black man. But this was politics, where Cahill was known as a no-holds-barred fighter. Cahill held out his hand. He was going to finish this un-diplomatic intrusion into his evening. 'Mr Nkomo, it is the policy of my colleagues in the EEC not to meddle in the private, internal affairs of sovereign states. I will be assuring Mr Mugabe that we look forward to working with him. It would be totally inappropriate to speculate on his internal relationships.'

Nkomo took his hand without moving closer. 'You will do what I say, Senator. I have already ensured I will be immediately informed of the content of your discussions.'

'Good night, Mr Nkomo.' Cahill went to withdraw his hand, but Nkomo held it, stepping right up against him. For a moment,

Mulligan thought the angry black man was going to hit his senator and fleetingly wondered what he should do.

'Senator!' Nkomo spat the word into Cahill's upturned face. 'I can guess what is in the travel bag from your sister's farm!'

Nkomo let Cahill go. Mulligan did not know if he had pushed him, or had Cahill stepped away, but the result was the same. Cahill fell backwards over the edge of the armchair and landed into it, legs shooting upwards, the colour draining from his face. Nkomo spoke at Mulligan. 'As you are aware, Mr Mulligan, our laws on the export of currency and valuables are very strict. The goods of all would-be smugglers are confiscated. Harsh prison sentences are meted out. I would appreciate you reminding your senator of this as you prepare him for his meeting with "prime minister" Mugabe.'

Cahill stayed in the chair, pretending to tie his lace.

'And now, Mr Mulligan, perhaps you would accompany me to the foyer so that I can answer any questions you might have.' Nkomo left the room without another word.

Waiting for the lift, never seeming so slow to arrive before, Mulligan listened to Nkomo inhale and exhale. He did not relish getting into the confined space with this very angry man. When the lift door closed, he felt a big hand grip his shoulder. 'I'm sorry about that, John. But there is too much at stake. I was not exaggerating with Cahill. There is too much to lose if Mugabe isn't warned off.' Nkomo seemed to deflate as he eased his hold on Mulligan's shoulder. 'John, you must ensure that Cahill impresses on Mugabe how seriously the West is taking the situation. If Mugabe believes you don't care...'

He tightened his grip again.

'... he will slaughter the Matabele people.' Nkomo's mouth curled in distaste. 'Cahill can have all the bags of diamonds he wants if he succeeds.'

Mulligan stepped quickly out of the lift, wanting to get away from the intensity of Nkomo, who moved in tandem with him. Nkomo stopped abruptly within inches of the lone white woman waiting in the foyer. They jumped back from each other in alarm.

Mulligan saw with relief that it was Patricia Lynch. He was just about to introduce them when she drew back her right arm and slapped Nkomo's shocked face with full force.

Mulligan crossed the floor impatiently, water wetting the carpet, shushing the imperious ringing of the phone that had disturbed his shower.

'Yes. Senator.' He wanted his voice to sound weary. It was, after all, only 6am. If he had been able to sleep after last night's developments, he would still be asleep, he told himself. Cahill did not bother to ask how Mulligan knew it was he calling and simply demanded to see him immediately, in his penthouse.

'I've taken the liberty of ordering you breakfast,' Cahill said, gesturing at the place settings for two people. He appeared to have recovered his composure. Wearing the pants of one of his dark pin-stripe suits and a crease-free white shirt, open at the neck, all he needed to do was slip on a jacket and tie and he could attend a formal meeting anywhere. Cahill poured the coffee.

'Mr. Mulligan.' From his tone there was no doubt that he blamed Mulligan for the turn of events. Seeming to concentrate on the task of precisely filling the cups, he spoke, almost daydreaming.

'When my mother died I was only nine years old. Mary effectively raised me. In fact, she refused to marry Eamonn Doran until I had finished my schooling. She wanted "to see me reared" as she would say herself. You know what it was like for farmers' second sons like Eamonn Doran. They were not in line for the inheritance and could not afford to buy land themselves. Eamonn and Mary moved to Africa in search of the famous "better" life.'

Cahill carefully dropped two cubes of sugar into his coffee. He studiously poured cream over the back of the spoon, and continued in a faraway voice.

'Up to recently we believed that is what they had found. When young Eddie went missing in action, they did not even tell us back home about it for weeks. Probably hoping against hope that he would turn up or something. We offered to come out, myself and my brothers and sisters, to join them in a ceremony of remembrance or whatever it is they call these things, but herself and Eamonn refused. Mary particularly. As you have seen, there's a whole load of unresolved issues in their, in her life now.'

While he spoke, Cahill had carefully sipped his coffee, sliced some of his bacon and butterred the fresh bread rolls that were the pride of the hotel. 'I would do anything to help my sister. Probably no more than you would yourself, Mr. Mulligan, if you were in the same situation. Anything.'

It was one of the best displays of deliberate casualness Mulligan had ever witnessed. Concentrating on what Cahill was saying, he mirrored his actions, not wanting to appear spellbound. He froze, the cup at his lips, when Cahill asked, 'If this fellow Nkomo is Matabele, isn't that what they call themselves, then does the other fellow, Charamba, belong to the rival gang? The Shona?'

Cahill was sneering over his words, trying to insult the two men in their absence.

'I imagine so.' Mulligan tried to sound as non-committal as possible, fearing where the point was going. Cahill put down his knife and fork and waited for Mulligan to do the same. Then the cross-examination began. Every detail of Mugabe's behaviour at the garden party was probed. Who spoke first between Charamba and Mugabe? How did they greet each other? How many other people did Mugabe embrace? Where was Nkomo during all this? Did Mugabe speak to him? Cahill repeated questions, confirming something for himself. Finally, he stopped abruptly. 'Thank you for your time, Mr Mulligan.'

His instincts told Mulligan to leave right now, but the words came out. 'The grapevine says that Nkomo is not exaggerating. If you do as he says, you can leave with the travel bag and maybe serve some greater good.'

Cahill replied contemptuously. 'Through Charamba, I am going to warn Mugabe that the Nkomo gang have asked the West to help them stamp out the little Marxist megalomaniac, and whatever else I imagine they might call him. I'm sure premier Mugabe will be very indebted to me, indebted enough to listen to my recommendation that they maintain strong links with the West.' Cahill wiped his lips with the large, starched table napkin. 'It's a way of killing two birds with one stone. Mugabe will be more benign towards me, and I'm sure the customs officers will not bother checking the luggage of such an important emissary of the EEC. Particularly one who has exposed their new boss's enemies.'

He threw the napkin onto the remnants of the breakfast. End of meeting. Mulligan went to leave, regretting he had ever asked. The knowledge of what Cahill was going to do made him an accomplice now. He walked quickly towards the door. Cahill spoke coldly. 'Nobody fucks with Gerry Cahill.'

Here they were again, Patricia Lynch told herself, driving around under the African sun. They were in an open-top jeep of the same vintage as the one they had shared at the field hospital in Biafra. She had agreed to let Nkomo drive her on her reconnaissance visit to the refugee camps and shanty towns that had sprung up around Salisbury. It was at the end of a long night's talking and recrimination that she had given in, not just because his advice that it would be safer and easier to be escorted made sense, but she also knew she did not want this man to simply walk out of her life again.

'I swear I didn't know my girlfriend in Canada was pregnant when I met you. She had not told me because she did not want me worrying too much and cutting short my assignment with the Red Cross in Biafra. When eventually I found out, after young Morgan was born, I just did not know what to do. My girlfriend was now the mother of my son, but I was in love with you. That's when I decided to join the cause in Rhodesia.'

He claimed it had taken him more than three years after leaving Patricia before he was able to re-start a relationship with his Canadian girlfriend, using the excuse of his involvement in the struggle for freedom to explain his lack of contact.

'I just did not want my son growing up not knowing who his father was. Eventually, after years of letter writing and phone calls, I persuaded her to move to southern Zambia, and we found that we had feelings for each other. Before we married, I told her about what had happened with you, as I wanted to make a clean break.'

She listened to him work his way through the time they had spent apart. He glossed over the war years and concentrated on his role at the hospital, his work for the new administration and his son. He did not discuss his current relationship with his wife and they steered around the fact that there was another woman in his life.

He asked about her and she talked in detail about her work, but told him little about herself. She did not tell him about the phone calls and the visit to his home in Bulawayo. It was too soon for that. Maybe she might not ever tell him. He seemed unaware of it. His wife appeared to have chosen, for her own reasons, not to inform him about it: yet. He wholly believed her pretext for being in Rhodesia: her alibi of a recce on behalf of the Irish aid agencies. Finally, in one of the lulls between them as they skirted around the core issue of their past and future relationship, he said, trying to appear nonchalant, 'I hope you have found the man you deserve.'

She was a little taken aback and opted to maintain his tone, 'Many, many.' They evaluated each other, breaking eye contact too soon, not wanting to expose their true feelings. He then brought the subject back to the safer ground of her work and her stated reason for being in Rhodesia.

'There can be no question of you visiting the shanty towns on your own. Think about it. Just how risky it would be for a white woman to appear alone among people who have been displaced from their homes by the white man's war.' She could see the sense of what he was saying, now that they were calmer again, acting very professionally, guarding against the emotional question.

She considered him as he concentrated on keeping the jeep on the dirt track. His face was thinner, making his cheekbones more pronounced, and his receding hair was grey at the temples. He appeared much older and had lost weight. Patricia did not know if it was her presence, or had he really developed a coldness? Where was the warmth he had exuded in the field hospital? She wanted to ask him about the war, but knew it was off bounds and was left speculating, had he served as a doctor or as a fighter?

The refugee camp they were now assessing was similar to what she had witnessed many times in the past: uneven laneways stretched haphazardly before them with little cabin-like structures no more than five feet in height, assembled loosely from sheets of corrugated iron, wood, hard plastic and cardboard. The front walls were made of some flexible material, an old blanket or a sheet of plastic, anything that could be rolled up or moved aside to form doorways to the patchwork boxes. The slanting roofs and sloping walls leaned against each other, as precariously balanced as houses made from a deck of cards. Inside each little structure sat at least one woman with a child at her breast or on her lap. Other children played in the limited space they could find between the unstable dwellings. There were no men to be seen. The women had a listlessness about them, thrown in little heaps, sheltering in whatever shade they could creep into, away from the midday sun.

But Patricia became aware of one difference immediately. She had been through so many refugee camps in her working life to be almost inured to the poverty, hunger, hopelessness and ever-present death. A common thread was the apathy of the refugees, no longer caring, their dignity already long lost. But here, through their lethargy, the women glared at Patricia and in turn at this black man whose every movement was attentive to her. The simmering resentment towards her was as humiliating as it was intimidating: humiliating because Patricia felt they could see through her charade and perceived, in the shared instinct of her sex, why she had come to their country.

She had always made a point of talking to the inmates of refugee camps, either through an interpreter or directly in her limited Swahili, as she wanted them to understand they had not been forgotten. But after only ten minutes she told Morgan Nkomo that she had seen enough, and they walked towards the un-gated entrance.

Searing pain flowed from her ear. She saw a turnip-like vegetable, putrid in places in the advanced stages of decay, fall in slow motion to the ground and embed itself in the mud at her feet. She knew, watching it fall, that she had been hit by this vegetable. Her brain told her to control herself as her body wilted, her knees sagging, shoulders drooping into her chest, head falling forward, she falling over. For the second time in her life the big man beside her picked her up, gathering her into his frame, shouting abuse or instructions at someone. She was not unconscious, but she could do nothing only watch the mud jump up and down before her as he carried her towards the jeep. Women at the front of their lean-to cabins, one with her hand to her mouth in horror, another arms akimbo in a serves-you-right pose. Morgan Nkomo placed her on the back of the jeep, half sitting up in the recovery position. She could feel his gentle fingers touching for cuts and swelling through her short hair. 'My Patricia, my Patricia,' he kept saying, expertly checking her skull. He placed something cold against the side of her head. The stinging pain was receding, a pulsing throb taking its place.

'It's OK, its OK,' she told him, trying to reassure him he was not to blame, taking his hand, telling him she was not seriously hurt, just shocked at the suddenness of the blow. A soldier with rifle at the ready positioned himself between them and the women who had gathered at the entrance to the camp. In her out-of-body experience, Patricia imagined what these hopeless women must be thinking now as they watched her African companion lift her hands to his face and cry into them, his head moving in time with his deep sobs.

*

'I think a quick dip is called for,' Tom Kennedy said as they stepped into the shade of the hotel foyer from the afternoon sun. They had spent a desultory day calling on various government offices, ostensibly trying to establish areas of co-operation between Ireland and the newly emerging Zimbabwe. With Mugabe's meeting in train, the rest of these appointments that Mulligan had managed to make from Dublin did not really matter to the Irish delegation. Both sides were going through the motions, the futility of the meetings underlined by the people they met, largely second-line management in the various public services and government ministries. They were all white, mostly English or of English extraction and, like Thompson in the Ministry of Agriculture, they were just biding their time, waiting to be sacked or sidelined. To a man, they were polite, genuinely interested, mystified as to what "poor Ireland" with its rampant unemployment had to offer asset-rich Rhodesia. They were curious about the "outside world" as they repeatedly called it. What sort of salaries were managers paid in the UK? Were jobs hard to find? How much would a decent semi-detached cost? Did they know anything about Australia?

In general, they professed an aversion to moving to South Africa, comparing it to moving from "the frying pan into the fire". Nobody spoke about the war or what had gone before. Their questions about England and Australia and a life elsewhere than in Rhodesia were couched in hypothetical terms. If a chap were to do this, or that, what could he expect?

Kennedy did most of the answering, and Mulligan concluded as he listened that he did not see the plight of these middle-aged men. In his healthy, optimistic youth, Kennedy did not realise these men really had nowhere to run where they would have anything like their current lifestyles, despite an internal war and being cut off from the outside world. Their time of servants and gardeners, of swimming pools, sundowners and barbecues, of guaranteed promotion because of the colour of their skin, was fading with the passing of each day. It was obvious from their at times even hurt comments that they did not see themselves as monopolising, but as developing, the country's wealth. They were shocked at the excesses of racial discrimination in South Africa and the United States and were proud of how fairly they treated the black population. In turn, black farm workers, black junior civil servants and black soldiers and police gave them their loyalty: proof indeed of how well they were treated.

Two of their hosts were Irish. One, a Protestant from 'Londonderry' had a little skirmish of words with Mulligan as they added and deleted the 'London' prefix to Derry; another, a Kerry man, who would have kept them all day talking about Gaelic football if they had let him. Mulligan let Kennedy do the talking, his mind more occupied with his early morning conversation with Cahill. Could he have done more to persuade Cahill to go along with Nkomo? Should he have insisted on knowing why Nkomo wanted to meet with Cahill? Maybe he could have tutored the big man to whom he had instinctively warmed on how to deal with his senator? If he had handled the situation better, perhaps Nkomo would not be in danger now. This feeling of responsibility for his actions was unsettling him. He had spent the past ten years writing reports no one was interested in and not caring in turn. That was how he liked it. Why all this conscience searching? Why should he care what happened to a man he hardly knew?

Just as Kennedy and Mulligan made arrangements to meet again after Kennedy's swim, Cahill moved towards them out of the shadows at the far end of the hotel foyer. Mulligan had not seen him but knew from the change in Kennedy's demeanour that Cahill must be about.

'Gentlemen, I have some good news. Minister Julius Charamba has invited us to one of his little soirées this evening.' Cahill concentrated on Kennedy. 'He will be sending a car for us at half five, giving you enough time to get in a bit of R and R before the evening's diplomacy.'

Mulligan felt his throat going dry. The deal was done. Cahill had already met Charamba. As a bonus for selling out Nkomo, Charamba was going to make up for his calculated insult at their previous meeting. They could all be buddy-buddy now that they had found a common enemy in Morgan Nkomo and the threat to the supremacy of Robert Mugabe. Cahill's tone underlined that this was an order, his use of the word "diplomacy" telling the two civil servants their presence was required on official business. Mulligan walked past him.

'By the way, Minister Charamba specifically requested me to ensure Mizz Lynch is in our party. Will you see to that Mr Mulligan? She seems to have disappeared.'

Patrick Moriarty was already sitting on the bench in Cecil Square, throwing crumbs to the pigeons. As soon as Mulligan sat down beside him, he scattered the remaining pieces of bread and rubbed his hands together.

'John, what's going on?'

Mulligan had to admire his directness. 'I take it you know about Cahill meeting Charamba?'

'A private tête-à-tête, no less. I wasn't invited.'

'I'm not surprised.'

'You know what they say, John, "birds of a feather…" '

'Patrick, Are you sure you want to hear this?'

'I didn't ask you to meet here without knowing what I might be getting into. Shoot.'

Mulligan told him about Nkomo coming to the room and the plan that Cahill had hatched overnight.

'Does your senator have any idea who he's meddling with?'

'Probably not. But as always with Cahill, he has his own agenda.'

'You know, John, UDI couldn't have ended soon enough for me. Patrick will be eighteen next month, so conscription loomed on one side but my biggest worry was that I didn't know how much longer I could have kept my lads from heading off into the bush. One of their uncles was killed only last year. Another is missing.'

Mulligan gave a long low whistle.

'It's pretty much an open secret that Daya's family were heavily involved in the resistance movement. Why, I think they probably saw me as a security risk in the ministry.'

'So that's why Charamba trusts you?'

'I think "trust" is an over-statement. I'm useful to him. For the moment. You see, my wife is from Bulawayo. It's looking like it could be more dangerous to be married to a Matabele woman under this new regime than it was under the last.'

As the policemen approached, Moriarty said loudly, 'And what was the score at half time?'

Mulligan talked about an imaginary hurling match, throwing in random snippets from any highlights of games that came to mind. The policemen's radios crackled as they strolled by, ignoring the two white men.

'John, the dogs in the street know that Morgan Nkomo is right. Mugabe is hell-bent on taking complete control and there's plenty of Charambas there to egg him on.'

'This really is a bit of a mess, isn't it?'

'You are so out of your depth, you wouldn't believe it.'

'It's too late now anyway. Cahill has briefed Charamba.'

'But there is one thing you can do.'

Mulligan waited, not wanting to anticipate Moriarty's request but knowing that the dilemma he had wrestled with all day was coming to a head.

'John, you must warn Morgan Nkomo. He is a decent man. If he knows the game is up, then he can head back to Bulawayo. He will be safe there; for a while at least.'

Moriarty brushed some crumbs from his lap. 'But whatever you do,' he whispered, impatient with Mulligan's unresponsiveness, 'keep my bloody name out of it.'

*

Patricia held the cold-water container to the side of her head as they drove away. The throbbing had receded. Now she just felt her ear glowing against the metal drinking bottle. Morgan Nkomo was hunched over the steering wheel. The depressing outer suburbia of lock-ups and factory buildings gave way to the countryside: the smooth, perfectly maintained road stretching like a ribbon across the parched earth, leading them towards little green shrubs, strewn patchily about at first and then closer together in denser swathes, giving way to trees sitting on green grass. She knew they were in an irrigation bowl of some great river or lake. He veered off the road and drove on a gravel path, climbing upwards, the wheels of the jeep scattering the stones. The steepness of the climb could be judged by the increasing pitter-patter of the pebbles against the underside of the jeep as the wheels dug into the ground. She gasped when they reached the top of the rise. Below them, reaching to the edge of the horizon, was the biggest stretch of inland water she had ever seen, blue and perfectly smooth, surrounded by lush grass and the foliage of well-irrigated trees.

In the moments after he switched off the engine the smaller noises made their presence heard: the nearby call of some bird; a far-off roar and animal shrieks of panic and pain; the tinkle of the engine as it cooled down. The details of the scene became apparent: huge flocks of waders feeding among the reeds, a motorboat carving through the glass-like water.

His hands eased their grip on the steering wheel and his breathing deepened. He spoke at the scene below them.

'Lake McIlwaine.'

She moved away from him in mock surprise. One of Morgan Nkomo's quirks she had loved was his refusal to use the colonial explorers' names for African landmarks such as Victoria Falls, insisting on calling it by its African name, Mosioatunya, or sometimes playing a game, using only the English translation, 'the smoke that thunders'.

'Lake McIlwaine?' she added for emphasis, unsure whether the unspoken communication was strong enough between them.

'It's OK,' he laughed, 'I haven't lost my values.' His hand swept across the picture framed by the windscreen. 'This lake does not predate the white man.' He smiled at her bewilderment. 'It was built in the fifties and is called after the civil engineer who came up with the idea.'

They laughed in a quiet, good-humoured way: the first real warmth between them in Rhodesia. He brought the canvas cover up over their heads and leaned back in his seat with a deep sigh, his eyes closed.

'I have never loved any woman as much as I love you.' He spoke the words upwards to the canvas. The silence refilled between them.

'Morgan.' She whispered his name, just once, stifling her tears. She held his eyes with hers. Her hands unbuttoned her shirt, exposing her bare breasts.

After witnessing Patricia Lynch slapping Morgan Nkomo's face, and the big man's reaction of shock and submission, arms partly outstretched in an unfinished embrace, Mulligan had stepped back into the lift and disappeared behind the joining doors. He was too much of an old hand to get embroiled in other people's lives and he had put two and two quickly together to figure out why Patricia had been so anxious to be part of the mission to Zimbabwe.

Mulligan was now having great difficulty persuading Patricia to accompany them to Charamba's garden party. She had other plans for the evening and she was not going to change them for that bollix Cahill, she vehemently told Mulligan. Suddenly, he saw a chink of light.

'Are you meeting Morgan Nkomo?'

Patricia tilted her head, silently saying, 'what's it to you?', but did not answer.

'Ask him to meet you there. Tell him I want to talk to him.'

'Mulligan, I hate it when you act as if you can see through me.

Don't be jumping to any conclusions as to why I'm here. Maybe I'm not meeting him.'

'Trust me, Patricia. I need to talk to him.'

The urgency in Mulligan's tone unsettled her. She stepped back into her room and Mulligan followed as she rooted through her small handbag and produced a slip of paper, squinting to read the phone number. The ringing was answered almost immediately by a muffled, male voice.

'Morgan, we might have to change our plans. The Irish team has been invited to some function at Charamba's place. John Mulligan wants you to meet him there.'

Mulligan listened as Nkomo said something to Patricia. He moved towards her, holding out his hand. Why wait, why not warn Nkomo now? Patricia handed the phone over to him resentfully.

'Morgan, how're you doing, John Mulligan here.' He hardly waited for Nkomo to reply. 'Morgan, that business from last night, there's been a significant development...'

'John! John!' Nkomo shouting his name down the line, forcing him to stop, was drowning his words out. 'John, my dear friend. Do not be so impatient. You can give me all your news later.'

Nkomo hung up. Mulligan held the burring phone to his ear, listening. Then he heard it, the tiny, almost indiscernible click. The phone was tapped.

'What's going on?' Patricia asked nervously as Mulligan replaced the receiver. He promised to tell her later and left the room before she could press him for more information.

Julius Charamba rushed across the lawn to greet Gerry Cahill. He welcomed each of the others in turn, giving a half bow to Patricia. 'Are you enjoying your visit to Zimbabwe, Miss Lynch?'

Patricia frowned, detecting his sarcasm. He did not wait for her answer and led the Irish party towards the centre of the garden where there was one woman talking to two men: Morgan Nkomo and the junior civil servant called William from Thompson's office. Cahill fell to the back, wanting the protection of the others on meeting Nkomo again. Charamba introduced Mulligan to the African woman, majestic in her native costume, and then with a sweep of his hand, said, '…and, of course, you know these two gentlemen.'

Charamba repeated the process with Kennedy, introducing Nkomo as well as the woman. Mulligan could see the game plan emerging, with Charamba again wanting to demonstrate how much he knew. Smiling broadly, he said, 'Senator, senator, excuse my manners,' in a pretence of apology for not introducing Cahill first, 'I don't think any of my friends have had the pleasure of meeting you before.' Cahill was uncomfortable, shaking hands with each person coolly, suspicious of Charamba.

'My manners, my manners,' Charamba gushed, 'excuse my terrible manners, Miss Lynch.' He introduced Patricia to the African woman, then to William beside her. 'William has a special interest in Ireland, Miss Lynch. He was taught by the Holy Ghost Fathers in primary school.' Letting William unwittingly keep Patricia from Morgan Nkomo, Charamba made no attempt to complete the introductions. The obvious way he was acting out his little game was disconcerting all the connected people present.

Cahill engaged the African woman in conversation, wanting to avoid contact with Nkomo. Mulligan joined the trio of Patricia, William and Charamba, anxious not to be seen to make his move too soon. Kennedy, innocent of the machinations, talked to Nkomo.

Mulligan saw Charamba slip away and wondered was he just imagining it or did the minister seem furtive?

Patrick Moriarty was at the far end of the garden, but when Mulligan waved in recognition the Irishman just continued talking to his wife and another African woman.

'Is that your contact in Charamba's office?' Patricia had seen Moriarty's reaction to Mulligan, and added, 'He doesn't seem too friendly.'

'I think I'd better talk to Morgan before Charamba gets back,' Mulligan whispered to her.

Nkomo and Kennedy were getting on well. The wine had loosened Kennedy's tongue and Mulligan was having difficulty giving him the hint to disappear.

'I think our good senator may need rescuing, Tom.'

Kennedy raised his glass in Cahill's direction, where it was obvious that if anyone needed rescuing it was the woman whose cleavage was mesmerising the senator, and laughed at Mulligan's joke. But a quick jerk of his head from Mulligan left him in no doubt that he was not wanted.

Patricia was waiting to break away from the now voluble William, anxious to hear what was going on. Nkomo's face was bent to within inches of Mulligan's, tiny nods of understanding punctuating what he was hearing as Mulligan spoke rapidly. She saw Charamba re-emerge from the house and stand on the veranda, his eyes fixed on the two men. She sensed that Charamba knew what Mulligan was saying and wanted to call out to warn them when the army lorry bulged through the well-tended hedging, soldiers in full combat fatigues jumping from the back through the dust being raised by the braking wheels. They silently encircled the garden, rifles at the ready, conversation petering out as people became aware of their presence.

Nkomo took Mulligan's elbow and guided him towards Patricia.

'John, make sure she does not do anything foolish.'

'Morgan, what is happening?' Her eyes widened in fear.

'Patricia. My Patricia. Please, please do what John Mulligan tells you.' Nkomo's voice was weak. 'It will be a comfort for me to know that at least you are safe.'

As Patricia moved to touch him, Nkomo stepped around her towards the approaching Charamba. The two men stopped within two feet of each other, Nkomo glaring defiantly down into Charamba's face, his fists clenched on taut arms pressing his anger into his body. The difference in height and size between them was remarkable, but Charamba arrogantly stood his ground.

Mulligan watched the politician confront the soldier. While Charamba had been availing of the UN scholarships, Nkomo had fought the fight for freedom in the bush of Rhodesia, but Mulligan could see the soldier was now outmanoeuvred. Suddenly, Nkomo broke away from the staring game with Charamba. For a moment, his shoulders appeared to sag. He glanced at Patricia but immediately away again, afraid that he might involve her. He then turned towards Cahill, confirming that he knew who had betrayed him. He held Cahill's eyes for a moment before the Irish senator started studying his feet. Then Morgan Nkomo marched directly at Julius Charamba, forcing him to move out of his way as he brushed past him.

The black officer, indistinguishable from the other soldiers but for the insignia on his green beret, was trying to appear at ease, hands joined behind his back, feet apart, as Nkomo came straight at him, his pace quickening. When he was just one step away from crashing into the young man, Nkomo stopped, pounding his feet together. The officer came to attention in response. The two men stood, bodies rigid, faces locked. Mulligan could hear the rumble of Nkomo's voice. The officer responded animatedly, shaking his head in answer, perhaps apologising for what he had to do to a fellow comrade in arms? Both extended their hands and formally finalised some agreement. Then they stepped back from each other and saluted. The officer sharply turned on his heels and Nkomo fell in beside him. The two, fellow officers now, marched side by side between the soldiers towards the gate.

Patricia moved, but Mulligan's restraining hand on her elbow stopped her. Everybody else remained perfectly still. Transfixed. Charamba, the victor, took centre stage in the space vacated by the officer and Nkomo and clapped his hands over his head.

'Comrades, comrades, our friend Morgan Nkomo has had to leave on urgent government business.' He waited, defying anyone to contradict him. 'Please forgive the interruption and enjoy the rest of the evening.'

Some of the groups immediately started talking again, wanting to ignore the implications of what they had seen. But Mulligan could see the pockets of silent fear: Charamba's public arrest of Nkomo a warning to them all.

Hoping to get some re-assurance from Patrick Moriarty, Mulligan checked around the garden but the Irishman and his Zimbabwean wife were nowhere to be seen.

Patricia hurried towards the gate, Mulligan trying to catch up with her. No one attempted to stop her, people deliberately turning the other way, not wanting to be a part of the next act of the unfolding drama. She half-walked, half-ran down the empty suburban street, its serenity restored. There was no trace of the army vehicles, no give-away clouds of dust, or fumes: not even someone to ask. Mulligan caught up with her when she stopped at the intersection, unsure of what to do next. He was breathless and gripped her bare elbow tightly before he spoke.

'This is not the time for heroics.'

Trying to ignore the pain from his tightening grip, she could smell the staleness of cigarettes, the closeness of his breath wetting the side of her face, when he whispered, 'Believe me, Patricia, this is not the time for a white woman to be arrested in Rhodesia.'

He stayed very close beside her, wheezing lightly, waiting for the words to penetrate. She was struck by the incongruity of him whispering on the empty street. An army jeep drove by, the soldiers in the open back leering at her. Mulligan and Patricia stared back, forcing them to turn away, except for one, who chillingly ogled Patricia until she could no longer see him. Mulligan felt her elbow go limp and eased his grip. She leaned against him. He slipped his arm around her shoulders, worried that she might faint. The first taxi he hailed stopped and the elderly black driver jumped out, his face full of concern. 'Is missus unwell?'

'Yes, I'm afraid so. Could you take us to Meikles?'

The anxious driver helped Mulligan settle Patricia into the car, holding her gently by the arm, fretting as he tried to help her without touching her too much. She slumped against Mulligan in the back seat.

'We will pass the hospital, sir, on the way to Meikles. Maybe we should stop there?'

'No. Thank you. We have medication at the hotel.'

The taxi-man drove quickly, even slipping around a corner through a red light. He brought the car right up to the door of the hotel and spoke urgently to one of the porters through his open window before he stopped. The porter sprang to life and rushed to open Mulligan's door. Whether it was the effect of the familiar surroundings of the hotel, or of the three men awkwardly trying to help her, but Patricia was suddenly upright and moving away from them. Mulligan was relieved to see her old self returning. He rushed after the driver who was closing the door of his cab as the taxi pulled away, extending a twenty-dollar note, wanting to over-tip, reaching out in gratitude. The car stopped. The driver held up his hand. 'No, no, sir. I am very happy to be of assistance. I pray your good wife makes a speedy recovery.' He rolled up his window to prevent further discussion about payment.

Mulligan insisted on escorting Patricia to her room. After she witnessing his failed attempt to warn Nkomo on the phone, he felt he had no choice but to be honest with her. Patricia listened, sitting on the bed, and when Mulligan finished she jumped up and stalked up and down the hotel bedroom, telling him of her year with Morgan Nkomo. Every few minutes she interrupted her story to plead, 'You must get Cahill to do something!'

He was uncomfortable listening to her, not wanting all this detail of her caring: she needing to tell him about the whole of her love for Nkomo, trying to convince him how important it was for someone to intercede. He was surprised to learn that Nkomo was a doctor, and when he said this she stopped, reflecting on his words.

'I know what you mean. I could see the hard exterior as well, almost like a shield.' She thought about her analysis, and added, 'It's something soldiers develop who have been in combat. I did not want to ask him about his time in the bush. Not yet, anyway.'

She gasped, realising she would never get another chance to ask Morgan Nkomo anything unless she could convince Cahill to intervene. The right word from him could get Nkomo expelled from the country. He would lose his homeland, but at least would have his life. Eventually she sat back down on the bed, wringing her hands, the tears welling and falling slowly. She switched off all the lights except for one beside the headboard.

Mulligan's silence summed up his helplessness. He welcomed the shadows, not wanting to witness her naked grief. She became perfectly still, her head bent, hands joined on her lap. He could hear her breathing deeply. When she appeared to have recovered her composure, he was impatient to leave, telling her gently that he must go as he scribbled his room number on the blotting paper on the writing desk. Checking the internal lock on the handle, he warned her not to answer her door to anyone. 'Absolutely no one!' He felt peculiar giving her orders, but she did not seem to care.

John Mulligan opened the small drinks cabinet. The bottles appeared as symbols of another time, a time of real freedom when he had the balls to tell the Cahills of this world where to get off. An unwanted memory crept into his consciousness and trampled about, reminding him of the real past, without the music and the mad fun, the 'craic'. Christmas Eve. The girls must have been only about six and three. He had gone into town to pick up the *pièce de résistance* of the Santa promise: two Barbie dolls that Kate had got the shop assistant to swear she would hold for one hour, a late delivery, being snapped up by frantic parents. Mission accomplished, he strolled down Grafton Street, free from the pressures of the last-minute shoppers. The crowded street was like the throng leaving Croke Park. Was it his imagination or did everyone seem to be walking against him? He even checked over his shoulder, verifying that the scrum of bodies was pushing both ways. At the junction with Harry Street, he slipped out of the cauldron and into McDaid's.

Negotiating the short distance down Waterloo Road, stopping to absorb the Christmas lights in an open-curtained window, he felt good, flushed with the warmth of the Christmas Eve companionship of the bars, a Munster final recaptured, more vivid in the telling. He was "pleased as Punch", having made a special effort to leave before closing time. Kate would appreciate that. The warm glow he now felt was extended towards her and his two daughters, probably still trying to get asleep, too excited by Santa's forthcoming visit.

At first she did not believe him. He found it difficult to believe it himself. He sat slumped in the chair, Kate standing over him, her urgent whispers trying to force him to remember. Where did he leave the dolls? Could he not remember where he had been? He could, but not when he last had the package with him. Nor did he want to reveal the journey from McDaid's to the Waterloo Bar: Davy Byrnes, the Horseshoe Bar (just for one), O'Donoghue's, Toner's, Doheny and Nesbitt's. Or was it the other way around? And, finally, into the Waterloo.

'If I remembered where I'd forgotten them then I wouldn't have forgotten them.' He felt his logic was impeccable, simply impeccable. Kate crying silently, the tears flowing freely down her cheeks. He knew she was crying for more than the lost dolls. She put on her coat. She would search through his haunts, she knew them all, she sobbed. He staggered to his feet and blocked the doorway, arms outstretched, a parody of the crucifixion. But it was his begging eyes that stopped her. It was all said in those. I know I'm a fool, but don't make me look like one. She reluctantly took off her coat, caring enough to want to avoid embarrassing him.

Typical Kate, she ensured the girls were unaware of the crisis. For years later they would boast about the Christmas when Santa came twice. She used the minor presents and the gifts from her parents to tide them over Christmas morning, and easily picked up two other Barbie dolls in an after-Christmas sale of a delivery that had arrived too late for the Santa frenzy.

Mulligan opened the window and craned out into the warm night, wanting some distraction, to exorcise the double guilt, from his distant past and from what he had witnessed earlier. There was no traffic in the street below, an unofficial curfew keeping the white people in their homes while the blacks were slowly coming to terms with the fact that the city now belonged to them. A sound of young men singing barely reached him.

'Zim zim zim-bab- waaayy'.

He did not have another drink that Christmas, but the damage was done, to the supposedly festive holiday and, yet again, to his marriage. Staying at home sober and edgy probably caused as many problems as his drinking. Kate slept with the girls, claiming they were afraid of the dark. Her conversation seemed to be a litany of complaints. The flat was too small. It would be nice if the girls could have rooms of their own. Remember the show house they were supposed to visit? Had he been passed over in the last round of overseas postings? Between the stinging questions, there were silences.

They each concentrated on the children, protection against the emptiness. He returned to work on the day before New Year's Eve, glad to escape the confinement. Then a chink of light entered the prison of their lives. The overseas assignment, to open an office in Zambia, would give them a chance to recapture the life and love they once shared. The money he would make would be enough to put a deposit on a house, so a major bone of contention in their marriage would be removed. The evening before he left for Lusaka, they had talked it up this way in their most civilised meal together in a year. It was almost like old times again. Kate still went to the girls' bedroom, but not before she whispered, 'We will make up for lost time in Lusaka.'

Mulligan waved the bottle of whiskey about, challenging the ghosts to stop him, and then spitefully lifted it to his mouth and drank in a flame of taste.

Cahill led the way to a table in the corner of the foyer without even asking Kennedy if he wanted to join him. An immaculately groomed waiter was waiting to take their order before they sat down. 'I think, Tom, a couple of G and T's would do very nicely.'

Kennedy could see the gracious mood coming on. 'Yes. Senator.'

'Enough of that "senator" bullshit at this hour of the night. Just call me Gerry.'

Tom Kennedy did not reply, silently cursing Mulligan for deserting him. The last thing he wanted was to be on the piss with 'Gerry'. A very large black woman approached the table as soon as the waiter had set down their drinks. She was bursting out of her dress, many sizes too small and too short for her heavy thighs. Her bright red lipstick was smeared, her thick lips appearing distorted.

'Manheru, good evening gentlemen.' The words chortled from her throat.

Cahill raised his hand, stopping her in her tracks. 'No. Thank you.' He said it firmly, without turning towards her. Not breaking her stride, she changed direction just enough to wobble by their table. Only a keen observer would have realised she had been approaching them before her advances were rejected.

'I think we can do better than that, eh Tom.'

Kennedy felt trapped, not knowing how he was going to extricate himself from the situation. He could feel the wine from Charamba's hospitality kicking in and was annoyed with himself for not refusing Cahill's invitation. They talked in short bursts, quickly exhausting each subject from hurling to television. Of course, that favourite topic of conversation for all Irish people, politics, was taboo between a politician and a civil servant. And Cahill's discomfiture during Nkomo's arrest had not been lost on Kennedy, so the real issue of the evening was also off-limits.

Tom Kennedy had just decided that he could leave when the two girls came towards them. They were both tall, almost of equal height, and both wore kimono style dresses with their shoulders bare. They walked with the grace of models, the lightness of the kimonos clinging to their figures, their right thighs being exposed in unison by the long slits in the dresses. The only thing reducing the extraordinary sophistication of their appearance was their unusual accessories - large canvas shoulder bags. The girl who came nearer to them was deep black with striking Negroid features. Her companion, in contrast, was no darker than a well-tanned Irish woman, her straight nose and high cheekbones revealing the Arab influence in her blood.

'Do you mind if we sit here?' the darker woman asked, pointing at the chairs at the opposite side of the low table. Kennedy had to admit that they were two of the most beautiful women he had ever seen. Cahill waved his arm to invite them into the seats and he leant over to Kennedy, stage whispering, 'The good-looking one is mine.'

Both women pouted at Cahill, acknowledging the compliment. The senator did most of the talking, spinning a long yarn about they being American businessmen working for Heinz. He introduced himself, describing Kennedy as 'my assistant', not able to let the pecking order be forgotten, even in this make-believe.

'You can just call us "Tom and Gerry" but this Gerry is no mouse,' Cahill told them but his joke about the cartoon characters was lost on the young women.

'I am Lucinda. This is Rebecca.' The darker of the women spoke very deliberately, as if testing the sounds of the names.

They asked Cahill to tell them more about America, about his houses, his cars and all the trappings of his imagined wealth which he outlined for them in a pseudo-American accent Irish people usually reserve for sneering at "returned Yanks". He even called them 'honey' from time to time. Power really must be an aphrodisiac, Kennedy remarked wryly to himself as both women hung on Cahill's every word. He shifted in his chair and was about to get up when Lucinda slid a box of matches across the polished table, inviting him to light her cigarette. She bent towards him, putting her free hand on Kennedy's knee, making sure he had an open view of her breasts hanging loose under her kimono. As she leant over his outstretched hand, she raised her eyes upwards, wordlessly letting him know, 'Just checking that you're checking'. Kennedy reddened. He could feel his defences crumbling.

He was a long way from home; no one was ever going to know the difference, he told himself as he crossed the hotel lobby to the reception desk and asked for both room keys. He was nervous, very nervous. Was the night porter going to reproach him for entertaining the prostitutes? Was he going to accuse them of bringing Meikles into disrepute? In his nervousness, he was imagining this aloof black man on the other side of the desk reading the thoughts of sex dancing in his brain.

Waiting for the keys, he watched the two women laughing with Cahill, titillating himself with how great a temptation he was facing. This was the perfect "occasion of sin", far from home, conscience dulled by a few drinks, with no one to know but Cahill who would be as compromised as he was. If the porter had any opinion on what was going on, he was not going to reveal it to Kennedy. The elderly man scrutinised the pigeon-holes, moving his finger across the rows of numbers.

'The penthouse, sir.' He handed the key over with a small flourish, using the term 'sir' without any irony. 'And room 102.' With the second key he gave Tom Kennedy a small slip of paper. Kennedy's brain was functioning slowly after the unaccustomed drinking and he quizzically fingered the note. 'A telephone message, sir. While you were out this evening.'

Kennedy leaned on the reception desk and gingerly opened the note, reading every word.

Meikles Hotel, Salisbury

Old world standards in new world luxury

Written on the dotted lines in a semi-printed script was the cryptic message, 'Row Nen sends his love.'

It took a few seconds for the phonetic spelling to register. Row Nen? And then, it dawned on him, a message from his wife, on behalf of their child. 'Ronan sends his love.' The laughing face of his three-year-old son was now wiping out all other images.

'Can I be of any further help, sir?'

'No. Yes. Please. Could I have some note paper.'

'I have a bad dose of the gawks,' he wrote, exhilarated with the crudeness, 'I will see you tomorrow.' He did not address it or sign it. Taking a dollar from his wallet he handed the slip of paper to the porter with instructions to give it to Cahill after five minutes. Without a backward glance, he walked quickly to the lift.

*

129

Mulligan sat with the empty whiskey noggin in his hand. Room Service must be gone to Scotland for the full size bottle he had ordered. He laughed out loud at his little joke, revelling in the almost forgotten feeling of the onset of drunkenness. He heard the characteristic knock on the door: a nervous tap, conveying the diffidence of servants. 'About bloody time!' He spoke towards the window, not bothering to turn around. The knocking was repeated, louder, more urgent.

'Tar isteach, come in, entrée.' The door opened. 'Just leave it on the table.'

The door closed again. No tip tonight, my friend. A pang of guilt was quickly dismissed by a surge of the bloody-mindedness that characterised the final years of his drinking. 'Fuck, fuck, fuck. Fuck you, Cahill.' He spoke aloud angrily out the window, the scene of Nkomo's arrest re-enacting itself.

There was a tiny sound of movement. He was about to ignore it when it was repeated, a gentle rustle and, definitely, someone breathing. He glanced over his shoulder without turning around, feeling foolish that his paranoia was finally getting the better of him. Turning away quickly, finding himself staring into his shocked face reflected in the windowpane, Mulligan was tempted to ignore his "little arrangement", nervously waiting on him, forgotten in the turmoil of the evening. He slowly faced her, not wanting to see her nakedness, but unable to take his eyes off her. The dress lay at her feet, a pool of yellow colour on the dull brown carpet. Slim legs accentuated her thighs, rounding out to enclose a neat mound of pubic hair. Her hands were at her sides, arms length, striking no pose, yet her small breasts stood firmly, nipples pointing tautly from darker circles. Long hair, making her seem older, framing her young girl's face, two child's eyes filled with trepidation. He did not want to see those eyes, only to simply drown in the beauty of her womanhood.

'She's only a child, you bastard,' he told himself, trying to shock himself back to reality, to responsibility, 'look at her face!'

'How old are you?' His voice was just a hoarse whisper. She did not seem to understand him, and opened the palms of her hands towards him, arms at her sides, gesturing her helplessness.

'How...old...are...you?' He knew she now understood, her expression wide in bewilderment.

'I am young, mister, really I am.' The tears filled her eyes, afraid of his rejection for being too old.

'Oh God, I know that. I know you are young.' He tried to inflect some gentleness into his voice, but felt too weary to do even that. She smiled in turn, not understanding his response and moved towards him, her diminutive figure accentuated as she stepped into his space. He put his hand out as one would to touch the head of a child who had stepped forward for approval. The wig slipping back from her forehead surprised him. His hand brushed over the bristle of her short, tufted hair, making him draw in his breath sharply in a rush of pleasure memories.

She moved closer to him. He could smell her womanhood and fresh sweat. His breathing was shallow and fast, fighting the madness, wanting desperately to lose the battle. His right hand remained on her head. She took his left hand, keenly looking up into his face, and placed it on her breast, reassured now with the effect she was having on this big white man. Mulligan breathed sharply through his nostrils as she sank to her knees, bringing the zip of his fly downwards. Her wig fell off and rested on her ankles like a furry animal. He placed his hands on the fuzzy tuftiness of her head, and groaned.

'Where the fuck are you going?' Cahill had walked out of the gents and now lurched in front of Kennedy, blocking his path to the lifts. He had been so busy writing his note, he had not checked to see where Cahill was, assuming he must be entertaining the girls.

'To bed, Sen...I mean Gerry.' Kennedy was annoyed to hear the tremor in his voice.

'I should have fucking known.' Cahill was getting indignant. 'The spineless little bollix has got cold feet. Afraid of a bit of black pussy.' Cahill snatched the piece of paper from Kennedy's hand and held it up to his face.

'Row...Nen...sends...his...love.' He read again, loudly. 'Why mister, loving, daddy Kennedy, Row Nen sends...'

Tom Kennedy grabbed Cahill's hand, twisting it quickly so that Cahill had to bend his knees to save his wrist from breaking. Kennedy twisted again. Cahill went down on one knee. Kennedy tightened his grip just enough to impress on the senator the amount of control he could exert. The telephone message quivered in Cahill's contorted hand. Kennedy deliberately took the slip of paper with his free left hand and placed it carefully in his shirt pocket.

'Go fuck yourself. Gerry!' He pushed Cahill's arm away from him as he released it, spitting at him, 'And you can stuff the fucking promotion. Gerry!'

Cahill stayed on one knee as the lift door closed. He slowly got up and checked himself in the full-length mirrors of the second lift, sitting open, waiting for the late-night stragglers. No one had seen what had happened. The services lobby was hidden from the main hotel area. Kennedy's lift was descending. The lanky bollix must be returning with an apology. Cahill waited self-righteously. The doors opened and a familiar figure stepped out. Well, well, now he'd let precious prude Kennedy find out what African pussy was really like.

Mulligan tightened his grip, bringing his hands down around her ears. Cupping her head, he lifted her gently to her feet. Her face below his filled with uncertainty. He felt thankful that his member was still in his pants, his arousal disappearing as he held without passion the face of this naked girl, this naked young girl, young enough to be his daughter. A flash of shiny bodies squirming in bathtime suds, shrieks of laughter bouncing off the tiled walls, filled his brain, to be swallowed by an overwhelming sense of loss. He had thrown it all away: those little moments of parenthood and domesticity that can only be created through patient time, that can never be manufactured in the regulated, planned visits that became his relationship with his two daughters. Saturday mornings on buses to Waterford, afternoons in cinemas or playgrounds, promising he would move down soon to be near them all the time, Kate waiting in the car at the bus stop while they repeatedly hugged goodbye.

'Get dressed. I'm too tired.' He spoke sharply, leaving her in no doubt this order was to be obeyed. The girl placed her arm across her breasts, bending defensively, moving her other arm to cover the rest of her nakedness. Crouching, she stepped towards the crumpled dress. Mulligan crossed the room. Staring at the wall, he held two twenty dollar notes in the open doorway, fanned out so that she could see how much she was being bribed to leave quickly. She ran past him, snatching the money, skipping into her sandals in the corridor. Mulligan leaned against the closed door, shutting his eyes, trying to contain the dam that was about to burst. He slid to the floor, bringing his face into his hands, tasting the saltiness of his tears, the relief as the floodgates opened, not feeling ashamed of himself for the first time in too many years. He had lost it all but, for once, tonight he had done the right thing. A deep sense of peace came over him. He remembered not the actual scene from long ago, but the feelings surrounding it, of snoozing in an armchair in the middle of the night as his colicky daughter finally went to sleep on his chest, their breathing becoming rhythmic. He could not distinguish which of the two girls was in the scene. Had it happened with both of them or was he just imagining it all?

Mulligan opened his eyes, reality returning. On the floor, in the middle of the room, a rat was about to attack. His stomach tightened. He was at almost eye level with the vermin, vulnerable to a spring at his throat. He waited, unable to breathe. The lifeless wig waited in turn. With a whoop, he jumped to his feet and kicked it against the wall.

*

133

Tom Kennedy undid the buttons of his shirt, trying to control the racing sensations, the high from flooring Cahill first giving way to grim satisfaction and then fear for his career; his agitation being fuelled by the image of Lucinda's breasts hanging into her dress. It would have been all so easy: two beautiful women, there for the taking. He felt the stirring in his crotch, yet again this evening, guiltily reminding him how willing he had been to surrender. He had never considered being unfaithful to his wife. In the six years together, it had never crossed his mind. He felt so above temptation he could not even share in the sly jokes that seemed to abound among his colleagues, the loaded references to the joys of Leeson Street and "French leave" when the trips abroad were being discussed. He had always felt vaguely superior in his faithfulness. It had even given him a kind of strength in dealing with Cahill, whose open womanising he despised.

Walking up and down in the confined space of the bedroom, he kept telling himself he was being too self-critical, trying to blame the drink rather than the beauty of the women for his almost fall from grace. He slipped off his pants and underpants, the coolness of the air tingling his body under the ceiling fan. When he heard the loud knock on the door, he realised there had been a persistent rapping somewhere in the background. Oh no, not Cahill! 'Hang on, hang on,' he called in as drowsy a voice as he could muster. He decided against the luxurious, white, hotel dressing gown and tied a bath towel around his waist instead, just to reinforce with Cahill that he was about to have a shower. Before he could say anything she had walked past him into the centre of the room. Even in his shock, he noted with relief the empty hotel corridor, before slamming the door to imagined prying eyes. She had already discarded her clothes. 'Mr Gerry tell me to say he send me.'

*

'Excuse me sir.' The voice spoke urgently out of the dark. It took Mulligan a moment to focus on where it was coming from before he saw the whites of the eyes of the very black man, dressed in black, who stepped out of the shadows. He could not tell what sort of uniform the man was wearing. Was he a policeman or hotel worker? Mulligan concluded that he was a hotel worker as he appeared nervous about giving an instruction. 'It's not advisable to venture from the hotel after dark.'

Mulligan stepped into the empty street, the sounds of the crickets helping to underline the absence of activity. He assessed the man's advice: hotel guests are never safe on streets. It was a standard cant: in Dublin, New York, London. Just imagine what they must tell people staying at the Europa Hotel in Belfast. 'OK. Thank you.'

The man retreated into the shadows. His job was done. It was not his place to argue. White men always did whatever they wanted anyway. He had smelt the whiskey: drunken white men were even worse.

Mulligan strode away from the hotel, wanting to leave behind his confusion of guilt and relief. The women, all his "little arrangements" had been a mistake. And tonight, that girl had been just too, too young. But the second bottle of whiskey, finally delivered by room service, had gone down the sink. On that count, at least, he had stumbled but not fallen. Coming back to Africa had been a mistake. He had assumed he had been cured of his weakness after what happened in Lusaka. At home in Dublin he had never thought of buying a prostitute, not even one of the black women, reputedly from Liverpool, who sporadically appeared on the canal banks. But he had no sooner arrived in Zimbabwe than the same old John Mulligan had surfaced. He stopped at the intersection, checking left and right on the deserted street, trying to decide which might be the better direction to take. Despite his dismissal of the watchman's advice, it had unsettled him. He wanted to stick close to the hotel.

Not for the first time since arriving in Salisbury, Mulligan had the feeling of stepping back in time. The shop fronts reminded him of Grafton Street in the sixties, evenings together with Kate as they strolled along, not paying too much heed to what was in the windows, talking earnestly together, constantly checking into the big-wheeled pram at their sleeping daughter. In those days there was so much to talk about with the civil rights movement sweeping across the world from the college campuses of the USA, to Paris, to Belfast and Dublin. The night after Nelson's Pillar was blown up they spent the whole evening talking in Irish and got very drunk in O'Donoghue's pub, keeping the child amused with crisps and orange. He knew it was not just the time-frozen fashions of Salisbury that brought Kate so much to mind.

In Africa, their marriage had finally ended in tragic farce. Not half as dramatic as the rumour that had seeped through the Department, claiming his wife had surprised him in bed with an African beauty, sometimes exaggerated further to two fabulous women, depending on who was telling and who was listening. But surprise him she did, standing at the shoulder of his former driver who was hitting back for the injustice done to him in the only way he knew how: the only way he could. Betrayed by his faithful driver, who had even helped him find alternative venues for his "little arrangements" when the insatiable Mulligan did not want to appear in the Lusaka International Hotel every evening. The silent, patient Zambian who ferried him from woman to woman, none of them professional prostitutes, just pretty girls working in government offices and shops, satisfied to get a generous taxi fare for spending an evening with a pleasant white man wanting only to have sex with them. In his bitter moments, Mulligan imagined it had not been just his driver's way of retaliating, but it had been the revenge of all the local men who looked the other way: Africa's revenge on yet another white man who could not resist the local charms.

Mulligan slowed, becoming aware there was someone very close to him. He had been too absorbed in the past when he should have been taking heed of the watchman's words of warning. He stopped and glanced over his shoulder. A young African was face to face with him, noses almost touching, both jerking away from collision. Behind the young man were four or five others. Two of them carried empty bottles held like shortened truncheons. The dark street appeared very quiet.

The woman was encouraged with the effect her nakedness was having on the apparently spellbound Kennedy. She took a step towards him, hell-bent on earning the money that Cahill had promised would be forthcoming from this shy white man. 'He say you like to rumpy pumpy but you very shy.'

Kennedy raised his hands. He had a crazy temptation to cover his eyes. Maybe she would then just disappear. 'No, no,' he heard himself pleading, 'there must be a misunderstanding.'

To add to her impact, she folded her arms behind her head in an attempt to thrust her breasts forward, creating a parody of the classic erotic description of a woman's nakedness: the triangle of her underarm and crotch hair were like three tufts of a badly made wig; the triangle of nipples to navel almost non-existent, her pendulous breasts nearly aligned with the button of her bloated belly; the triangle of crotch smothered into the fatness of her thighs. Her eyes to her lips were just a loose geometry, a statement of drunken - or maybe even syphilitic - craziness. Cahill, the bastard, had sent to his room the large prostitute he had so haughtily dismissed earlier. She moved towards Kennedy, undeterred, a giant, preying mantis. 'You can do whatever you want with me.' That bloody chortle again. Kennedy inwardly groaned, stretching his arms outwards at full length. She must keep her distance. He could smell the combination of fresh and stale sweat and what must be other men's spunk as she came closer. 'Maybe you like me to give you...' She licked her lips.

Kennedy followed the downward path of her eyes to see a faint bulge pressing against his towel skirt.

'For Christ's sake!' He spoke aloud, wanting to disown his reaction. The handle of the door pressed into his lower back. He had retreated as far as he could. She placed her left arm on his chest, leaning her bosom onto him, her breasts spreading themselves around his torso. Her right hand, gently, surprisingly gently, cupped his balls. He could feel the calluses. The silent debate was turning against him. It would be easy now to stop being so pure. She was in his room. Available. To do anything he wanted. He could ignore the smells of booze and sweat, and the whiff of sex from earlier clients, and just screw her any way he wanted. He could always disregard any comments, insist nothing had happened, and Cahill would have to assume the porter had stopped her or that she had got the room numbers mixed up. She squeezed his balls lightly and moved her left hand flatly over his abdomen, making him catch his breath. The towel slipped to the floor. She tested his bulging erection and leant forward, mouth open, the movement giving him a view of the cleavage of her backside. 'I think you like me to suck you.' She said it matter-of-factly, his passion diagnosed.

'No! Wait, Wait!' He whispered at her urgently. She took his prick in her mouth.

'Wait! Wait!'

She closed her lips tightly over his knob and sucked very hard.

'I want to fuck your ass. Let me get a Durex!' At first he thought she was not going to let him go, but she slowly withdrew her head, the top of his prick emerging, being drawn through the tight orifice of her lips.

'I want to fuck your ass!'

She let his prick pop from her mouth and sighed, 'You white men.'

A weariness crossed her face.

'Where was you in the war?' The young man was standing so close to him he could feel the warmth of his breath with the cider smell of apples. Two of his companions flanked the youth. Mulligan was aware of the others circling him, taking position. One of them laughed nervously. Something hard prodded into his back, and Mulligan knew he was going to have very little time for explanations.

'The war, the fucking war, I'll tell you where I wah uz during the fucking war.' He leaned towards the youth nearest to him and spoke into his face, forcing him to smell the whiskey on his breath. 'I was up in Belfast shooting the fucking British army bashtards.' He swayed distinctly, hoping his drunken act was convincing enough to save his life. Their surprised faces said it all. They were at a complete loss at this unexpected response. The ringleader drew back, restoring some of his space to Mulligan. 'Where you from?'

Mulligan stepped out of the loose circle. Now he could see the entire group: and they him. It was vitally important to hold their attention. The last thing he wanted was a cider bottle on the back of his head from one of the gang who was not following his play-acting.

'Ireland, gentlemen, I am from Ireland. The first country to strike a blow against imperial Britain and where the noble struggle for freedom is going on to this very day.'

He let his eyes drift towards the ground, pretending to be too drunk, and concentrated on the six pairs of feet, all in open, ill-fitting sandals below loose green pants. He was on their side. They must not see his fear. He had once seen a German tourist shot in Lusaka, struggling to remove his ring after he had handed over his wallet, camera and watch. As the tourist lay on the ground dying, his attacker hacked his ring finger off with a penknife.

These young men were probably in the bush fighting a few months ago. Now they wanted what was theirs: quickly.

'What part of Ireland?' The question was asked from one of the youths furthest away from him.

'Tipperary.' No point in dampening their curiosity by truthfully naming his obscure home county. Everyone had heard of 'Tipperary'.

'Do you know Father Kelly?'

Mulligan shifted his position so that he could see his interrogator, evidently a product of a Catholic education.

'No, but I know Bishop Lamont.'

In unison they moved away from him. There was a collective shifting of feet. He embellished the lie.

'He was one of my teachers in Ireland before he moved to Africa.' Here I am, he thought, a middle-aged agnostic, in deepest Africa, needing the help of the Irish clergy.

'Bishop Lamont is a true friend of the people of Umtali, a true friend of Zimbabwe,' his latest interrogator stated. Mulligan raised his hand, a show of farewell. 'Nice to meet you lads, but I'd better be getting back to my hotel.'

The ringleader laughed, a row of white teeth flashing in the light from the shop window. The others joined in. 'But Mr Irishman, we want you to tell us about the Irish Republican Army.'

The group moved towards the recessed doorway of a furniture shop. Mulligan was harbouring some vague notion that he might be able to escape despite what his brain told him: he could never outrun these young men who had the poised explosiveness of trained athletes. He followed them into the tiled entrance, moving deliberately to where the admirer of Bishop Lamont was squatting on his haunches and crouched down beside him.

'I'm sure you must be very happy the war is over?' Mulligan addressed the question to no one in particular, just wanting to take the focus away from himself. All except the ringleader suddenly appeared to be very interested in the tiles on which they sat and squatted.

'Yes. It is good. But the white men are still here.' The ringleader threw his arm out to capture the European name over the shop door. 'We will wait and see.' The deeper intonation of his voice in the cavern of the recessed entrance gave his words an added significance.

Assessing them in the brighter light, Mulligan realised just how young they were: barely fifteen or sixteen, no older than his own children. Despite his vulnerable position, Mulligan's core feeling changed from one of fear to sympathy. These boys had known nothing but the domination of the Smith regime. Had they spent their lives in the bush? Were they war orphans or veterans? What horrors had they witnessed or perpetrated? Mulligan leaned back against the window and let his legs slide outwards so that he was sitting on the ground. 'I will say the same thing to you as I said to Comrade Mugabe only yesterday.'

All eyes were on him. His heavy name-dropping was having some effect.

'You must be patient. As we know in Ireland, these things take time.' Mulligan was warming to his subject, and he proceeded to give them a potted history of Ireland, focusing on the parallels with Africa: people being expelled from their land, the suppression of the language, the famine and finally the insurrection and war of independence. He decided not to mention the civil war; there was no point in depressing them with insights into the fate of newly-independent countries. A fate that Morgan Nkomo believed awaited their dream.

Most of the questions were addressed through the ringleader who jerked his thumb towards Mulligan while the others laughed. Mulligan waited, bemused.

'My brother wants to know what did you do with the black people?'

'In Ireland, we Irish, we were the black people.'

The ringleader laughed loudly and placed his hand on Mulligan's shoulder, squeezing him warmly. 'And your Doctor Ian Paisley, I think he is Mister Ian Smith's brother.'

Mulligan covered the man's hand with his and pressed emphatically. Now, they understood each other. Suddenly the history lesson was over and it was like playing twenty questions. They wanted to know about the world outside of Africa. Had he ever met Martin Luther King? Why did the Beatles call themselves beetles? Was the 'Little Red Book' really red? Why did women burn their bras? Do the Americans think they own the moon? Does everyone hate Maggie Thatcher? The questions were based on a hotchpotch of knowledge, stemming from pop and political opinion moulded from radio broadcasts that most likely did not emanate from the BBC World Service. It was obvious that they did not distinguish between the USA and Britain: both icons of wealth and imperialism.

Mulligan fed them answers, sometimes true, sometimes based

on what he felt they might like to hear. There was no point in disillusioning them about the new country they felt they were about to inherit, no point in asking where would they be in the queue for jobs in the liberated Zimbabwe? In showing them that what little they had to offer had already been given in the bush. That Zimbabwe was not short of well-educated émigrés, all too eager to come home after years of exile. Where would these young men be in ten years time? Waiting for the farms they had been promised?

Mulligan exaggeratedly checked his watch, but did not refer to the time. The ringleader shifted position. 'I think we have detained our visitor from Ireland for too long.'

His influence was strong enough to get them all quickly to their feet. Mulligan creaked his way upward to join them, the ringleader taking his elbow. 'Before we finish, we will sing a song for our Irishman friend.' He spoke solemnly.

The young men appeared uncertain. Then one of them took the lead, backed by the others, including one or two tuneless contributors. It was the same air as the woman's song at the airport, but sung more slowly, almost mournfully. The young male voices echoed around the empty shop doorway. Near the end, the ringleader quickened the pace, wanting to draw them out of their soulful reverie, and stepping out into the street he raised his clenched fist in the air, imitated by the others punching upwards into the dark, emphasising the loud climax.

'Zim-zim-zimbabwe.'

'Zim-zim-zimbabwe.'

'Zim-zim-zimbabwe.'

They stopped suddenly, their echoes fading away.

'Now, we would like to hear a song from you.' The statement was an order, not a request. Mulligan took the ringleader's fist and sang.

'T'was down by the glen side...'

As he sang he pumped the ringleader's arm, his big hand enveloping the other's clenched fist like a sliotar, squeezing it tightly as the words from his schooldays came back to him.

'I met an old woma a a a n
a plucking young nettles
ne'er saw I was comennnnnn...'

Tom Kennedy tried to grab the towel from the floor but the prostitute was too fast for him, leaving him with no choice. Leaping naked from the room, he pulled the door shut and frantically checked the empty corridor. What next, what next! The door shook in its frame as she wrenched the handle, accompanied by a screeching roar. Halfway down the passageway he could see the emergency exit. The concrete stairs tore at his feet. Stubbing his toe on the second last step, he rushed onto Mulligan's floor. He ran up and down the anonymous corridor looking for inspiration, resisting the temptation to call out Mulligan's name. A man and woman laughed in a nearby room. Oh shit! Up another flight of stairs. Patricia, Patricia. What was her number? He hopped from foot to foot in the cold stairwell, forcing the memory from his subconscious. Such inspiration! He almost laughed in relief. What had she said that morning checking in? 'I think hotels should not use the number thirteen in case they upset superstitious guests.'

More collected now, he poked his head into the empty corridor, checking left and right. Placing his left hand over his genitalia he tiptoed, keeping close to the wall, counting off the room numbers. He knocked once on Patricia's door and waited, placing his right hand over his left, fingers spread to cover as much of his nakedness as possible. Maybe she was asleep? More, louder, sharper knocks, discretion abandoned. The lift door opened and a woman's voice broke the silence. He scuttled back towards the emergency exit. The woman and her companion seemed to round the corner just as he reached the stairwell. He leaned heavily against the fire door to keep it from being opened from the corridor, pressing against it for an age until he was certain no one was coming.

*

Cahill was chuckling to himself at the little scheme he had hatched for Kennedy. He was propped between the two women, a hand on each of their backsides, treating himself to the loveliest contradiction of all, the yielding firmness of a woman's derriere.

The girls appeared to be having a good time: at least Lucinda was, who snuggled closer to him, filling his nostrils with the smell of perfume. Rebecca was intense, nervous, clutching her canvas satchel tightly under her left arm. All three of them were contemplating the scene in the elevator mirror. Cahill whistled at his reflection. This was every man's fantasy and he was living it here and now, two women, one as beautiful as the other, and he was going to fuck them both. Maybe he would get them to put on a little exhibition, a sort of appetiser. He gripped their buttocks with his fingers outspread, digging into their flesh, steering them away from the door of his penthouse. Lucinda wiggled, resisting the pressure.

'What you doing?' Her voice was angry.

Gerry Cahill released them with a light push, lifting his arms to the sky. 'Ladies, ladies, we have the whole rooftop to ourselves.'

He had heard the anger in Lucinda's voice and wanted to mollify them, to coax them to share in the glorious feeling he had of being alive in the African night.

'Let's go skinny dipping.'

'But Mr Gerry, we want to see your big penthouse.' Lucinda's voice had an air of pleading. He drunkenly inspected the kidney shaped pool, a deeper shadow against the surrounding tiles, comprehending that it was covered by a blue rubber sheet, annoyed at having his plan thwarted.

'We go indoors.' He could feel the dampness on his ear as she spoke to him in a throaty whisper. She took his hand and pressed it onto her breast, her nipple rigid under the flimsy material. She held his right hand on her left breast and backed in the direction of the penthouse door, where the other girl waited, even more appealing in her nervousness. Cahill gripped Lucinda's breast tightly, stopping her backward walk. She winced, a momentary anxiety crossed her face, but then she laughed, not wanting to annoy him. Cahill could feel the power he had over her. His erection bursting against his pants, he moved closer to her, taking her right breast tightly in his left hand. He gripped her and brought her forward, right up close so that she could feel his erection, moving her in a firm, slow tempo, out to the edge of the roof, overlooking the white lights of the silent city. She took his rhythm and emphasised the push of her right thigh into his crotch, pressing his member. He was reading her game plan. She was trying to steer him towards the penthouse. Will she ever give up? He pressed his groin against her, leaning back his upper torso so as to maintain the firmness of the grip on her breasts. She kept her elbows tightly locked into her sides, using only her hips on his hardness.

The sound came up from the street through the clear, cooling air, each word held crisply, echoing from the valley of the buildings.

'T'was down by the glen side

I met an old woma a a a n...'

Cahill stopped, rhythm broken, and peered in disbelief into the shadows below.

'a plucking young nettles

ne'er saw I was comennnnnn...'

Listening to the next badly sung verse, his grip on her breasts eased and she could feel the hardness drain from his erection. She pressed against him.

'Let's go to the penthouse.' Despite her attempt at coquettishness, there was an urgency in her voice.

He could feel the stirring in his groin again. He would fuck her now, quickly, finish it off, get rid of his lust and get rid of these women.

'Glorio, glorio, to the bould Fenian men...'

The voice was louder now, the singer warming to his song. He released his grip on her breasts, interest waning. Fighting his distractedness, she pressed against him, bringing his thigh deep between her legs. Slipping his arm around her slim waist and drawing her hips against his, she guided him towards the penthouse: lovers to a tryst. Rebecca moved out of the shadow of the doorway to let them enter together. He stopped and took one step towards the rooftop wall, speaking each word with equal emphasis into the street below: 'Fuck... you... Mulligan.'

Inserting the key in the door, he spoke over his shoulder in a dismissive tone at Mulligan's intrusion, 'You drunken piss artist!'

Patricia Lynch was standing at the gate of the compound, the woman and boy watching her expectantly. Suddenly an army lorry ploughed to a stop beside her, granules of earth spattering her bare feet, soldiers jumping through the plume of dust, grabbing the boy, who was crying open-mouthed, not at his mother, but at Patricia: no words coming out. She awoke with a sudden jerk. It was all a dream, just a nightmare. But even through her semi-consciousness she knew something was wrong. Something awful and evil had happened. Slowly recovering from her stupor, she realised she must have fallen asleep. Sleep? At a time like this? She saw herself from outside, sprawled on the bed. 'Is this all I am going to do in Rhodesia?' she asked herself, 'Retreat to the bed in every predicament like some pitiful little girl?' She continued to berate herself, forcing her self-pity away with her anger. Why allow Mulligan restrain her? What was all this falling down in the street about? Far bigger crises than this were part of her job, where her decisions meant life or death for countless men, women and children. She knew what she must do, despite Mulligan's warning to stay indoors. Face up to Cahill right now. Go to his room. Let him know she meant business turning up in the middle of the night. Threaten to tell all on their return to Dublin.

When she put on the light, a mad woman stared out at her from the mirror. She could not challenge Cahill like this. It would be too easy for him to dismiss her. Splashing the water from the cold tap onto her face again and again, taking comfort in the mild shocks as she collected her thoughts. She decided to change into her black jeans and T-shirt, the clothes in which she always felt most comfortable and confident. Just as the shirt covered her head there was an urgent knocking on the door. She froze. Before she could react, there was another. Immediately followed by a loud bang. She could not move, her arms caught in the short sleeves.

Another bang.

The soldiers in her dream were at the door. Her stomach tightened. She felt her sphincter muscle grip, and for an awful moment she feared she was going to soil herself. She had seen the results of soldiers' brutality enough to know what was going to happen to her. The door banged again. She saw the young officer saluting Morgan Nkomo, Cahill's leering face, Charamba's smugness. Anger welled up inside her. She was not going to hide. Pulling the tee shirt sharply over her face, moving silently, she tiptoed across the room and jerked the door wide open to show them she was not afraid. The empty corridor was a shock to her: an anonymous passageway with its lines of mute doors. Somewhere a woman laughed, breaking her trance, and without further hesitation she slipped the key into her pocket and ran to the lift. Time to sort out Cahill.

'You must be a very wealthy man, Mr Gerry,' Lucinda said over her shoulder as the two women walked around the sumptuous penthouse, checking out every detail.

'Where is the, the restroom?' She tested the American word before coquettishly adding, 'Mr Gerry.'

Cahill laughed and started unbuttoning his shirt as they both went towards the door of the bathroom. He draped his pants over the back of a chair, throwing his underpants and socks underneath. Facing the bathroom door, he waited, arms akimbo, savouring the throb of his tumescence. He smirked down at his bulging member, sharing a private joke with little Gerry. Lucinda emerged, totally naked,

147

making Cahill draw in his breath at the magnificence of her beauty. Black beauty. Totally naked except, incongruously, for the satchel under her left arm. She moved towards him, smiling. Extending her right arm, she took his member in her hand, firmly holding him, leading him towards the bed. He glanced sideways to see Rebecca emerge from the bathroom. Her face was strained. She was naked also, her right arm partly covering her beautiful breasts as she reached across into the satchel. What is it with these girls and their satchels? Before the thought could take hold, Lucinda refocused his attention with a gentle tug on his penis. But she was not smiling. Her eyes were cold as ice, her face hideously distorted in a look of pure loathing. He recoiled as from a blow, but Lucinda's grip on his penis tightened. There was a rustling sound to his left from the other girl. Lucinda glanced towards Rebecca. He followed on reflex but, too late. A flash of steel. Instinctively he raised his left arm.

Below him in the concrete stairwell a door slammed and boots clattered up the steps. Kennedy covered the next flight upwards in two strides and burst onto the rooftop. The lights were on in Cahill's penthouse. Sounds of movement inside made him almost cry with relief. At least the fucker was awake. This is all your fault you bastard, he screamed to himself as he banged repeatedly on the door: no need for discretion now at this isolated penthouse. Silence. He felt a grim satisfaction that he just might have interrupted Cahill's bit of fun. The door sprang open. A naked woman shot past him, then another, both carrying small bundles of clothes as they ran towards the door Kennedy had just come through: Lucinda and Rebecca, as naked as he was. He really was pissed off with Cahill's jokes.

*

Mulligan finished and waited, letting the young man withdraw his fist. He thought he could hear a not too distant siren and prayed the police would come rushing down the street to rescue him from this knife-edge charade. The young men were uncertain. After an expanded time delay, stretched by his fear, the youth furthest away moved towards him. He was the smallest, but had a massive pair of shoulders and bulging forearms; tribal markings created darker, vertical grooves on his left cheek. He stood directly in front of Mulligan, his brow furrowed in puzzlement, trying to figure out the Irishman. The others had stepped back. It was apparent now who really was the ringleader.

'White man!'

Mulligan tensed for the knife in his ribs. Were his efforts about to be brushed aside? The youth's face was straining for words. 'White man! We forgive you!'

There was the shortest of silences before the others laughed and roared, taking the lead from the imprimatur of their leader. The gregarious young man, who Mulligan had assumed was the ringleader, grabbed him by the wrist, singing again, Zim zim zimbabwaay, Zim zim zimbabwaay, all the time raising and lowering Mulligan's arm, saluting the newborn country. The real ringleader marched away. Their celebrations over, the others followed emptily. The singer stopped abruptly, giving one last, silent, push upwards to Mulligan's' hand. He led Mulligan down the street in the opposite direction. Rounding the corner, Mulligan was amazed to see the hotel just across the road. He had not realised how close he was to base. At the front of the building were two police cars with a Mercedes in a line between them and an empty army lorry double-parked outside the last vehicle. Mulligan's new friend touched his shoulder. 'Be careful on the streets of Salisbury at night,' he whispered.

Mulligan smiled as the young man stroked his own face with his free left hand, acknowledging Mulligan's long beard.

'We know you was not a Rhodesian army officer, but others…'
He shrugged, the words trailing off.

'Chisarai. Stay well.' He blended into the shadows, laughing
quietly.

The door to Cahill's penthouse was wide open. Patricia waited,
uncertain of her next move. From the street below she heard the
sounds from her nightmare: trucks screeching to a halt, soldiers'
boots beating off the concrete, authoritative voices barking out
orders. Has Cahill been arrested as well? Did the authorities know
about his intended smuggling?

She rapped on the open door with her knuckles and stepped into
the short corridor, not waiting for an answer. She could hear another
sound, but was not sure whether it was animal or human. A repeated
'ah, ah'.

Kennedy was standing in the centre of the room, completely
naked, his hands frozen about six inches from his face, wanting to
cover his eyes but unable to complete the movement. He was
twitching, making the 'ah' sound. She got the smell of fresh faeces
and instinctively scanned Kennedy's buttocks. He was clean. Then
she got another smell. Unmistakable. Less acrid than the smell of the
faeces, but stronger now that it penetrated her nostrils. It was the
smell of fresh blood that she could now see: on the carpets, on the
walls, the ceiling: sprays of red spatters, everywhere.

Oh my God, has Kennedy killed Cahill? Her overwhelming
feeling was sympathy for the young man, his athleticism apparent on
his trim body, standing in front of her, paralysed except for the shiver
of his head as he tried to release the sound from his throat. She
silently moved towards him and placed her hand on the tip of his
elbow. Tom Kennedy screamed, high pitched, moving upwards from
octave to octave until it seemed his larynx would be torn out by the
sharpness, rising on his toes to follow the sound upwards. And then,

nothing. No more air left. No more sound. He stretched on his tiptoes for what seemed like an eternity before crumpling to the ground, revealing to Patricia what had shocked him.

The stream of puke gushed from her gaping mouth, drowning the screams trying to escape from her throat. She placed her hands on her knees, retching every last drop. Some of the yellow slime landed on Kennedy's head at her feet, further matting his sweat-drenched hair. Incongruously, she considered the mess and how difficult it would be for someone to clean up the place. Kennedy rolled fully on his back and opened his mouth to scream again. No sound. She heard a tiny rattle and instinctively followed the noise to Cahill, praying that it had not come from him. It must have been from the back of Kennedy's throat, she reassured herself, examining his mouth opening and closing, like a fish gasping for oxygen. She willed Kennedy to repeat the tiny rattle gurgle, a diminished version of a familiar sound from her nursing days, but she could not even hear him breathe, his speechless mouthing providing a welcome diversion.

She realised an awareness of water cascading, falling through the stepped glacial pools of her childhood swims, holding the blissful summers' days forever in her aural senses. She closed her eyes momentarily, letting the feeling wash over her, relieved to break from the proof of Cahill's agony filling every corner of the room. She walked towards the source of the noise behind the partially open bathroom door. The water from the shower had cleaned to pristine whiteness one area of the bath, sluicing a channel through the diluted redness. She instinctively crossed the bathroom, her sandals squelching as the blood tried to glue them to the tiles, and shut off the shower, freeing up her senses so that she could absorb the message in red writing on the mirror.

'Justice'

The words were a printed scrawl, sloping upwards from left to right.

'for'

She had seen the whole sentence at a glance, but was working through it now, bitter-sweetly.

'Morgan Nko'

She bent over and smeared her finger in the red treacle at her feet. One of her sandals slipped off, stuck to the bathroom floor, as she moved towards the mirror. She could feel the glue of the blood on her bare foot as she walked. She leant across the hand basin and with great, satisfying, care, wrote, 'm...o'.

She stepped back, approving of her work, and the work of Cahill's executioners, their deeds matching her darkest wishes. Patricia Lynch grimly read the message aloud, listening to the words soak into the white tiles until every morsel of sound had been absorbed.

'Justice for Morgan Nkomo.'

Mulligan remained under the shadow of a palm tree decorating the forecourt of the hotel, the danger from the youths replaced by foreboding that the presence of the police and army was connected to the Irish delegation. Had they come to arrest Patricia because of her links to Nkomo? It would be messy, particularly as she did not have diplomatic status, but he felt confident he could deal with it. Or had Nkomo won whatever power struggle was taking place with Charamba and was Cahill under arrest? Now, that would be really messy, but he told himself it was only wishful thinking. He smoked a cigarette, fully, to the very end, using the deep draughts of smoke to slow down his racing thoughts. Each drag made a beacon of the lighted cigarette end, and he was well aware any protection provided by the shadows was being totally wiped out. But he had decided hiding was not an option. There was nowhere to run. In a few minutes he would have to walk into the bright hotel lights and deal with whatever had to be dealt with. He knew, standing under the tree, some denouement had been reached, for himself, if not for the others.

The memory of earlier in the evening, when he managed to stop drinking, when he behaved half decently towards the young girl, filled him with a satisfying elation. He had taken control. Now, as he reflected on his encounter with the young men, he realised it was this knowledge of being in charge that had given him the strength to direct the situation. A week ago he would have just surrendered to his predicament, courting whatever fate was going to be inflicted upon him. Surrender, as he had done so many times in the past: to his drinking, to his lust, where he risked his health, his reputation and his marriage. He had destroyed every stem of esteem that his driver had for him as he used him as his pimp, and ruined the loyal, dignified, Zambian's life in the process.

The locked away incident came hurtling through his thoughts. Mulligan could feel himself blushing as the memory and all its attendant feelings took over. Peter. Peter Sithole, his Zambian driver, had only ever once revealed what he thought of Mulligan's philandering.

They were returning from one of his arrangements, Mulligan sipping from a hip flask of whiskey, aimlessly watching the mixture of red tile and galvanised roofing in the poor, outer suburb of Lusaka. Suddenly, he spotted a familiar street name. 'Are we near where you live, Peter?' The driver answered monosyllabically.

'I'd like to visit your house.' This was a boundary Mulligan should not cross, that he would not have crossed sober. Peter slouched over the wheel.

He swigged from the flask, the usual bad-temperedness after one of his assignations finding a new direction. 'Yes, yes, Peter. You're hardly ashamed of me, are you?'

Part of him could hear himself, a bully and a boor, but his self-destructiveness had too strong a hold on him. Peter silently left the main road, driving through a series of uneven avenues. He blew the horn for too long at children playing in the street, leaving them cowering as they passed. The car stopped in front of a small wooden house, distinguished from the others by the evenness of the two-feet high hedgerow surrounding a patch of dusty earth. There was no clutter in the garden or on the porch where two hanging baskets trailed red, rose-like flowers to the ground. Mulligan quickly got out of the car, not waiting for Peter to do his driver's thing and open the door for him, wanting to retrieve the situation. A stout, grey haired woman, wringing her hands as if she were drying them, opened the door.

'Mr Ambassador, this is my wife.'

Mulligan partly bowed and extended his hand. 'Mrs. Sithole, I am very pleased to meet you.'

He was determined now to make this potentially disastrous situation into a success. Mrs. Sithole led the way and Peter followed Mulligan. The front doorway led right into a living room, bright and airy. In the corner was a bookshelf with a collection of old hardbacks on the lower shelves and above them the paperbacks that Mulligan had passed on to Peter, assuming he was more interested in selling than reading them.

'Forgive this intrusion, Mrs. Sithole. We were in the neighbourhood and Peter insisted on showing me your beautiful home.'

Husband and wife exchanged a quick glance, acknowledging to each other this was a lie and Mulligan knew exactly what they were communicating. He declined the offer of tea and, after some very stilted chit-chat, used the excuse of a remembered appointment. His hand was almost on the door, wanting to end this intrusion, when it burst open and two figures tumbled into the room. Their mother called out their names, and then she spoke rapidly to her two daughters. Mulligan could not identify which of the many Zambian languages she was using as the two girls gathered their composure. Their school uniforms, incongruous on their young women's figures, underscored their likeness as twins. The only difference between them was that one had removed her school tie. Obviously they had run down the road on seeing the car, assuming their father had managed to borrow it for an hour. The girls curtsied as Mulligan shook hands with them, but both said 'pleased to meet you' in an assured, confident, manner. Mulligan guessed they might have been as old as nineteen or twenty, their father's income letting them finish their secondary education.

Massaging his neck on the headrest of the car in relief, Mulligan weighed up the outcome. Things had not gone too badly. He had left with lots of smiles and repeated handshakes all round. Peter seemed to have calmed down. Mulligan sucked a peppermint and idly examined the back of the driver's head, trying to read his thoughts, to empathise with the position he had forced on his dutiful employee. The edgy over-warmth of Mrs Sithole reminding him of the priests' visits to his mother's house, collecting their dues, his mother clucking about them, covering her nervousness with repeated offers of tea.

Peter opened the car door and they stood close together. Mulligan was tempted to shake his hand. That would have been enough. The wordless apology would have been accepted. Instead, he heard what was genuinely meant as an innocent remark coming from his mouth. 'You have very beautiful daughters.'

Peter recoiled, straining the door on its hinge. He pulled his shoulders back and his neck reached out of his starched white collar.

'They are MY daughters.'

Mulligan could hear the anger and incredulity in his voice.

'But Peter, I only meant...'

The magnitude of Peter's misinterpretation of the remark dawned on them both simultaneously.

'Mr Mulligan. Sir. I'm so sorry sir. I didn't mean...'

'Maybe you're right, Peter, to see me as just some womanising bastard.'

The driver started to cry.

'No sir. No sir. You're a good man sir.' Peter's voice was trembling. 'You are a generous employer. Please sir. My family will be lost without your job. Please sir, I didn't mean...'

Mulligan walked away without any further words spoken between them. Later that evening he sent Peter a letter by messenger saying that his services were no longer required, enclosing a month's wages, paid for from his own pocket so that the Department would believe his claim of pilfering.

Peter had exacted his revenge. Not of a mind to be paid off. Did he imagine that maybe he might get his so-important job back by running to Kate? Bringing her to the Lusaka International Hotel to witness Mulligan's infidelity. What had Peter done afterwards? Could he have secured another half-decent job without a reference? Had his daughters been able to continue their schooling?

Mulligan dragged deeply on the cigarette. He knew what he must do. Maybe in some bizarre way atone for the wrong against Peter Sithole and his family by standing up for Morgan Nkomo. He would go and confront Cahill. Force him to intervene. Even threaten not to be an accomplice to his intended smuggling. Get Nkomo expelled back to Canada: anywhere out of this country. He strode into the hotel lobby, ignoring the two soldiers at the entrance who watched him without reaction. As he waited for the lift, Charamba appeared. The soldiers had not been inattentive after all.

'Mr Mulligan. How fortunate to meet you here.' Behind Charamba was a black army sergeant.

'Minister Charamba?' Mulligan pretended to be surprised. Charamba wordlessly shepherded him into the lift and repeatedly pressed the button for the top floor. Charamba took his arm and guided him down the corridor towards the exit for the penthouse.

'I'm afraid, Mr Mulligan, there's been a dreadful incident.' He gripped Mulligan tightly when he used the word 'incident'. Mulligan inclined his head towards him, waiting to hear more, but Charamba propelled him with the words, 'Perhaps I should let you see for yourself.'

They moved up the narrow stairway in single file, Charamba leading the way. Mulligan stepped onto the hotel roof, above the streetlights, seeing the countless stars in the clear African sky. As he adjusted to the darkness, Mulligan saw figures spread around, many of them holding rifles at the ready. There appeared to be a mixture of soldiers and police. A white policeman with crew cut hair was standing a short distance from the doorway, in the well of its light. He moved away as Charamba approached and lit a cigarette, his palms cupping the flame becoming momentarily translucent, and then said something to his white colleague. They both laughed.

Charamba spoke conspiratorially to the NCO at his shoulder. Even in the seconds available to assimilate the scene, Mulligan could see the hostility between the white police and black soldiers. It was also apparent that the blacks were in charge.

Mulligan saw Tom Kennedy, wearing what appeared to be a sheet, talking to a number of soldiers. Then he realised the person standing next to Kennedy, with an arm around his waist, was Patricia Lynch. He was about to go over to them when the army sergeant pointed that he should stay with Charamba. Two soldiers outside the door of the penthouse made way for them. Charamba stopped and whispered to Mulligan, 'This will not be pretty. But I consider it best that you know what happened and then we can decide what needs to be done.'

Charamba stepped aside to let Mulligan enter the room. A lamp in the corner had been knocked over but its bulb was still working, casting a garish light across a line of carpet where bright red was mixed with something brownish. On the floor were two canvas satchels, dropped within inches of each other. Cahill's body was propped against the headboard, almost sitting upright, his chin drooping, deep gashes distorting the shape of his skull, the blood from his neck matting the hair on his chest. His legs had been spread to expose a huge bloodstain at his groin and two machetes were crossed between his feet. His right arm, covered in deep gashes, lay across his abdomen. Mulligan felt nothing, immersed at the revulsion of the scene, each second bringing more detail: Cahill's left forearm, attached by just a sliver of tendon, hanging over the side of the bed: on the floor, almost at Mulligan's feet, a scrotal blob and string of flesh caught on the edge of the arc of light from the fallen lamp.

With a sweep of his eyes taking in the spattered walls and ceiling, the army sergeant spoke matter-of-factly, 'Obviously there was quite a struggle, even after they chopped his arms.'

Mulligan imagined the flailing wrists spattering blood all over the room.

'His attackers were prepared for this amount of bloodshed.' The sergeant indicated the floor. From the middle of the room there was a trail of blood, even some distinct footsteps, leading towards the bathroom. Mulligan also saw dark patches of water, and he realised these passed under his feet and led out of the penthouse. The soldier moved towards the bathroom and lightly kicked the door more open with his boot. The sides of the bath were covered in blood. A white channel had been cut through the base, little rivulets of red trying to refill it as they snaked down the sides. 'It appears his attackers showered themselves here. They left in a hurry with their fresh clothes when your colleague, Mr Kennedy, disturbed them. At this stage we know they were female, but we cannot get a lot more from Mr Kennedy.' The sergeant added, indicating the mirror opposite the bath, 'We think the attackers may have mistaken Senator Cahill for a Rhodesian politician.'

'Justice for' was scrawled in blood on the mirror, the letters clearly visible over an indecipherable smudge. Mulligan spoke aloud, 'Justice for…' His subconscious finished the message, but he dared not speak the words, preferring instead to hear Charamba's voice giving them a plausible excuse they could all live with.

'There is a lot of anger in Zimbabwe in the aftermath of the war.' Charamba spoke evenly, making the statement as neutral as possible. 'Many people have been hurt. It will take some time before everyone feels avenged.'

The three men moved back to where they had entered the penthouse suite and took up the same positions, with the horrible view of Cahill's blood-covered corpse propped in a grotesque parody of someone sitting up. His attackers had gone to great effort to ensure the lump of stain between his legs was visible to all who would have to visit this scene.

'I hope he died quickly.' Mulligan spoke to no one in particular. He breathed a deep sigh, feeling his composure draining away, not wanting his detachment from the scene, from Cahill's mutilated body, to desert him now.

'I hope so.' The words were spoken gently by the army sergeant. 'Isn't that what we all pray for?'

*

Charamba sat on one of the two chairs in Mulligan's room, facing Patricia Lynch and Tom Kennedy sitting on the same side of the bed. Mulligan leaned against the wall, deliberately keeping out of Charamba's line of sight. He wanted to be able to observe, not allow Charamba complete control by having the three of them lined up in front of him like recalcitrant children for this "conference" they had been told to attend. Kennedy was dressed and appeared composed. Patricia had also detoured to change out of her blood and faeces-stained sandals. Throwing them into the waste disposal bin in her bathroom, she had sat on the edge of the bath, letting the cold water run over her feet, trying to see a way forward. Had all leverage died with Cahill?

Charamba leaned back on the chair, arms arched over his head, fingertips on fingertips, gathering his thoughts into the cage of his hands.

'My thanks to you all for joining me here. And thank you, Mr Mulligan, for the use of your room.'

No one spoke in reply. Mulligan gave a small snort. Thank you, indeed! Did they have any choice?

'This is a most unfortunate turn of events. Just when we were making such progress.' Charamba pressed his fingertips to his temples.

'I think it is in no one's interest that what happened here tonight is discussed elsewhere. It would be very embarrassing for the Irish government - and their European friends - for one of your distinguished emissaries to be killed in such compromising circumstances...' Charamba waited again, letting the enormity of the situation strike home. '...and very hurtful for poor Gerry Cahill's lovely wife, who has suffered enough.'

Charamba added in response to Mulligan's grimace, 'not to mention his sister in Rhodesia,' driving home just how much he knew. 'While you were preparing to assemble here we checked the penthouse carefully and we have discovered another possible motive for the attack. It appears that some of Senator Cahill's personal luggage may be missing. Two women were seen running from the hotel with a small overnight bag.'

Kennedy broke from his examination of the carpet. 'But...' Before he could say another word, a vital witness to the naked girls carrying nothing but small bundles of clothes, Mulligan said, 'Really!'

It was obvious from his tone that he wanted Charamba to know he did not believe him, but he did not want Kennedy to get into a war of truth or lies: not with all the odds stacked against him.

Charamba directed his answer at Mulligan. 'Yes. Mr Mulligan. Really!'

Knowing he had the upper hand, Charamba continued, 'Of course, we have no way of knowing precisely what is missing. Unless, that is, any of you can help us.'

Only Kennedy met his look, not realising the full extent of the game he was playing.

'I have spoken with,' Charamba was searching for the right word, 'with the authorities. There is general agreement that we can arrange an honourable death for Senator Cahill.'

Having established his position on the missing bag, he had changed his tone to that of conspirator. 'We know he was a keen jogger, so perhaps a heart attack while out exercising could be the cause of his untimely death?' He waited for the others to react to his plan.

'We need to have an excuse not to open the coffin.' Mulligan spoke the words flatly, then snorted, 'Some fucking heart attack.'

'Yes.' Kennedy agreed with Mulligan, 'yes,' warming to the conspiracy role, 'we need a car accident or something.'

'A car accident.' Charamba clapped, a schoolteacher encouraging a diligent student. 'How resourceful of you, Mr Kennedy. A bad car accident. With a fire, perhaps? Is that what you have in mind, Mr Kennedy.'

Kennedy shrugged, knowing he was being ridiculed. Patricia Lynch continued staring at the floor, not wanting to be drawn into this game. Charamba leaned back on the chair, his hands behind his head, talking to the ceiling. 'Of course, you may ask, why am I -

why are we - so concerned about Senator Cahill's reputation.' He waited for an answer. Then he closed his eyes, emphasising to them how carefully he was choosing his words.

'Zimbabwe has come through a long and difficult struggle. We are near the end. At times we felt the Western powers could have done more to help us, to speed our journey towards independence. Towards freedom. Now that we are near the end, it is important Comrade Mugabe is not constrained in what he needs to do to make one unified country out of this great land. To overcome the tribal differences that have impeded it in the past, that were only temporarily put aside in our fight against the common enemy.'

Charamba checked that everyone was listening to him. 'It is important to us that the West does not interfere as we take the necessary action to create a unified state. I know you have been hearing malicious rumours regarding Comrade Mugabe's intentions, Mr Mulligan. I know some treacherous people in our midst, fuelled by tribal jealousy, have been suggesting to you that the Shona and Matabele may not be able to co-operate in building a great new country. It will be useful to us that you report back to your European and American friends the findings of Senator Cahill before his untimely death. This report will help them understand that it will be the actions of Comrade Mugabe, and no one else, that will secure lasting stability in this country. In the whole southern region of this great continent.'

Charamba's face was deadly serious: no more game playing: he had set out the terms of the deal; there would be no negotiating. After all, he had all the aces.

Mulligan appeared to be having some huge internal conflict. To finish his private debate for him, Charamba added, his hand on the doorknob, 'I look forward to you sharing this draft report with me, Mr Mulligan. I'm sure Mr Kennedy will help you prepare it.'

On hearing his name mentioned, Kennedy glanced at Mulligan, who just shrugged resignedly before turning towards the window. 'So that's it,' Mulligan said aloud to his reflection in the glass, wanting to spell out what Charamba was offering. 'In return for protecting Cahill's and the Irish government's reputation from a disastrously embarrassing situation, we must report that Mugabe should be supported-or at least not hindered-in whatever action he is going to take.'

Mulligan and Charamba sized up each other in their reflections.

'Morgan Nkomo was not being alarmist.' Mulligan watched himself speak out the words, a stranger on a television screen. 'The war is not over yet, isn't that so Minister. Mugabe is not going to share power with his one-time ally in the struggle for freedom, Joshua Nkomo.'

'That, Mr Mulligan, is it in a nutshell.' Charamba's reflection replied. He appeared genuinely pleased with himself, and added, 'as you would say in Ireland.'

Mulligan shrugged and moved away from the window. 'I suppose we don't have much choice.'

Tom Kennedy gave a grimace that Mulligan took for agreement. Patricia Lynch appeared to be ignoring them. Charamba clapped his hands. 'We must get to work. Much needs to be done.'

Patricia jumped up and stepped forward. 'What about Morgan Nkomo?'

Charamba acted surprised. 'Ah, that Mr. Nkomo. I had forgotten you had such a great interest in the welfare of my colleague.' He spoke deliberately. 'Mr. Nkomo had to return urgently to his wife and son in Bulawayo.'

Patricia reddened.

'Miss Lynch.' Charamba sounded irritated. 'If you really care for Morgan Nkomo, then you should think about the safety of his family. I will give you my word...'

'Your bloody word!' Moving closer, she roared at him again, 'Your bloody word!'

He stepped back, controlling himself from raising his arms in protection.

'I will do better, Miss Lynch.'

Mulligan watched the cruel satisfaction as another lever for their loyalty became apparent to Charamba.

'I will place the safety of his wife and son, who I believe you have met, in your hands, Miss Lynch.' A sneer touched his lips. 'His wife will ring you on your return to Ireland to assure you of her well-being.'

The sockets of Patricia's eyes deepened as the colour drained from her cheeks. She knew Charamba had her outmanoeuvred.

'In time she will ring you again from Canada where she will return in due course. Your co-operation will ensure their safety.' Charamba smirked, another part of his jigsaw complete. 'We would not, after all, want to do anything to harm Canadian citizens.'

'But what about Morgan Nkomo?' This time her words came out as a plea. Charamba shrugged and opened his palms.

They worked through the remainder of the night, Kennedy largely going along with Mulligan's dictation, writing the report out longhand. Charamba had wanted to get it typed, but Mulligan convinced him it would undermine the authenticity of the document if they were seen to entrust an internal Departmental memo to a secretary provided by the hotel. Charamba digested this point carefully and did not press the matter any further. Mulligan was surprised at the lengths he was now prepared to go to ensure the credibility of the cover up. All he wanted was to wrap this mess up as neatly as possible. There was also a surprising feeling of what he grimly described to Tom Kennedy as 'patriotism': wanting to ensure nothing would embarrass his country. The feeling that hit him when he expelled the young girl from his bedroom kept resurging. He was in control again.

Just after 6am Irish time, he made the call to Dublin. He was direct and brief when he finally got through the drowsy international telephone operators to Brian O'Grady, the emergency liaison officer at the Department, and listened blankly to O'Grady's low whistle and small laugh.

'For Christ's sake...Cahill...the auld bollix,' was the reaction echoing through the line from Dublin, formalities being unnecessary between the former drinking companions. Mulligan checked if Charamba had heard the remark, but the minister appeared absorbed in his report reading.

'Yes. Regretfully Senator Cahill is no longer with us. Ar dheis Dé go raibh a anam.' He was signalling to Brian O'Grady that the phone call was being listened to by someone with enough Irish to understand 'may He rest in peace,' so resorting to the unofficial secret code of the Department of Foreign Affairs, the Irish language, was not an option.

'We don't know where Senator Cahill was going, but he was in a single vehicle accident and his car went on fire.'

'Is there anything you need me to do?'

'No, the Rhodesian-Zimbabwean authorities appear to have everything under control and they are assembling the full facts, as they say.'

'OK. If you hear anything else, give me a call back by twelve. We'll tell the family and give it to RTE for the one o'clock.'

'Don't do anything with the media till I get back to you. I want to make sure his sister who is here in Rhodesia hears it from me first.'

As Mulligan hung up, Charamba carefully folded the report.

'I will return these to you later.' Charamba left the room briskly.

'I wonder, Tom, who else needs to approve our interpretation of events, and how many photocopies are going to be kept in Salisbury?'

'I'm still a bit lost. What did Cahill do to deserve that?'

'You know, Tom, this might sound a bit heartless, but I'm starving. Let's get some breakfast.'

'And to think I was tempted...'

'I'd keep that to yourself if I were you.'

'Oh, thank God. That's all I can say. Thank God. I can't wait to get home.'

Charamba returned about two hours later and took a vacant chair at the table where the Irish were dawdling over breakfast. 'As I promised you earlier, I am now able to give you more official details of Senator Cahill's death. It appears he went for a visit to the country, I presume perhaps to see some friends, when his taxi left the road and overturned. Witnesses have told us it immediately burst into flames and we have been informed that Senator Cahill and the taxi driver died in the inferno.' Mulligan checked Patricia's reaction. She was expressionless, not seeming to appreciate the implications of Charamba's addition of a second crash victim.

'Mr Mulligan, as soon as we know what the situation is in Dublin, and you have informed the Doran family, we will be breaking the story on our national radio. I understand there will be some TV footage on the news this evening.'

Charamba knocked on Mulligan's bedroom door and opened it without waiting for an answer. He crossed the room and switched on the TV while Mulligan continued to lie on the bed, his head resting on his hands. He had been awake for nearly an hour, but felt too drained to move, content to slowly replay the week's events, trying to figure out what moves, if any, were left. Cahill was dead. His sister's lifetime savings were gone, probably stolen by Charamba. Their mission was in tatters. Morgan Nkomo was missing, very likely dead. If Nkomo was right, Mugabe was about to order a major bloodbath of the Matabele people, and the Irish delegation would be part of a conspiracy of inaction.

Charamba pulled the chair away from the writing bureau and leaned over to turn up the sound on the TV.

'I know you will be pleased with the coverage, Mr Mulligan.' He spoke again, ignoring Mulligan's truculence. 'We are anxious to ensure that you can see how well we are fulfilling our side of the bargain.'

The newsreader appeared on screen without a signature

introduction and the lead item was the death of the Irish senator, with footage of the burnt-out car and then of two body bags being loaded into a military ambulance. Mulligan thought was it his imagination, or was one of the body bags noticeably larger than the other? The gory scene gave way to a shot of Charamba, seated at a table and flanked by one of the officials who had been present the first time they had met and Patrick Moriarty. All looked suitably mournful as the camera panned across their faces, the voiceover giving more details of the Irish delegation's itinerary. Again, Mulligan did not know if his paranoia was running riot, but he felt that Moriarty's face was held on screen longer than the others. As his screen persona passed on the regrets of the Zimbabwean people to all concerned in close up, Charamba leaned over and switched off the TV.

'I thought involving Patrick was a nice touch.'

Mulligan swung his legs off the bed as Charamba stood up and replied, 'Yes. Indeed.' He was intent on keeping his voice as neutral as possible, afraid that anything he might say could further jeopardise Moriarty and his family.

Charamba did not appear to notice his non-committal answer. 'You will be contacted shortly about the arrangements for your departure. I will personally accompany our precious cargo to the airport.'

'Did you...' Mulligan was trying to pick his words carefully, knowing he could ask only one question, but needing so many answers. 'About Cahill...' He let the words hang in the silent room. They studied each other. A man's laughter filtered through the hotel corridor and voices passed by the door. Charamba, a puzzled expression crinkling his face, said wearily, 'We had already bought off your Senator Cahill. We did not need to kill him.' Then he added in an annoyed tone, ' In fact, it has been quite inconvenient.'

Mulligan did not reply, sensing it was best to let the silence be filled.

'Who knows who killed him. Maybe it was a freak incident. Maybe Senator Cahill had made enemies in Zimbabwe.'

Charamba assessed Mulligan's reaction, and then added, 'Your guess is as good as mine, Mr Mulligan. But we did not have any part in Senator Cahill's murder.' At that Charamba extended his hand. Mulligan wavered, just enough for Charamba to notice, who moved his hand slightly from the wrist, a tiny repeat of the invitation. When Mulligan accepted, Charamba gave him the charming smile he had greeted him with when they met at the barbecue and gripped his hand firmly, moving closer for emphasis, 'If we wanted to kill any of you Irish, we would have killed you.'

Mulligan was trying to establish how seriously to take him.

'We knew Cahill's price.' Disengaging from the handshake, Charamba reached into the breast pocket of his shirt and, with a small flourish, handed Mulligan a blue envelope.

'We did not know yours, Mr. Mulligan.'

'Come in.' Mulligan called out the words without moving from the bed, resisting the temptation to add, 'everybody else is doing so.'

Tom Kennedy stepped from the hallway into the gloom, leaving the door open, silhouetting him against the light from the corridor. 'I've been cooped up all day. I'm going down to the bar.'

Kennedy's voice had a firmness that Mulligan had not heard before. He was simply stating a fact, not asking for Mulligan's approval.

'I'll see you there.' Just before the light from the corridor was cut off, Mulligan called out, 'Will you get Patricia?'

He had to admit, Kennedy was right. This was not the time for hiding in rooms. It would also add to the credibility of their story if they put in an appearance in the bar. He lifted the letter lying on his chest and tore it into small pieces, wanting to get rid of it in the dark, trying to obliterate the words from his memory.

'Dear Gerry,

Things are very desperate. We would leave tomorrow morning

167

but Eamonn will not face home penniless. We do not know where to turn.

Remember us in your prayers.
Your loving sister,
Mary'

Mulligan dropped the shreds of paper down the toilet and flushed it, watched them bobbing about against the stream of water, refusing to go away. He peed on top of the fragments while the cistern refilled, flushing it again, talking aloud towards the cascade of water as he washed his hands. 'I'm sorry folks, but in every war there are winners and losers and I'm afraid...'

Just as he pulled the cord to extinguish the mirror light, he grunted at the tired, middle-aged man staring back at him, not wanting any more of his scrutiny.

Judge Bradshaw, even more flushed than usual, and the newspaperman, Seán Kirby, were sitting at a table at the opposite end of the bar, keeping the entrance under observation. They stood when the Irish delegation entered, leaving them in no doubt they were waiting for them. Mulligan submitted to the handshakes and the expressions of sympathy, introducing Patricia to Kirby.

'We heard earlier today at the paper, but the hotel insisted you were tied up when we rang,' Seán Kirby offered by way of explanation for their unannounced presence.

'It was Seán told me.' The judge spoke bitterly. 'No one seems to bother telling my office what's going on anymore.'

'Oh that's not true, Bob,' the journalist gently corrected him, but his voice sounded unconvincing.

Patricia ordered a large brandy, studiously ignoring Mulligan's silent attempt to warn her to be careful. The others were sympathetic towards her moroseness, assuming she was in shock at the news of Cahill's death. Conversation was desultory. Mulligan told them the story he had prepared.

'The senator wanted to see some more of the country. He always disliked "minders", so he headed off on his own,' Mulligan told them, a sprinkle of truth useful in holding the fabric of lies together.

'And he always did what he wanted. He could be very stubborn.' Mulligan's audience assumed this was a compliment to the dead man, stubbornness having been a respected trait of the white community in Rhodesia.

A sombreness descended on the little gathering, broken only by the sound of the ice being swirled nervously by Judge Bradshaw in his whiskey tumbler. It was the newspaperman who spoke next, moving the slice of lemon around the rim of his water glass as he chose his words.

'We saw Gerry Cahill as a sort of lifeline: as someone in the outside world who was sympathetic to our predicament.'

The judge vigorously agreed. 'Maybe you might think us naive, Mr Mulligan. You are an experienced civil servant and know more than most that there is only so much one man can do.'

Accepting that Mulligan was holding back, Kirby added, 'We don't seem to have many friends left in the "outside world".' He snorted harshly, marking his understatement. Bradshaw slumped further into his chair. Patricia grimly slugged back the remains of her second double brandy, and Mulligan feared there was an onslaught coming.

Bradshaw and Kirby rose in unison and Mulligan turned to see Mary and Eamonn Doran standing uncertainly at the door of the bar, appearing very lost, grief distorting their faces when they recognised the small Irish gathering.

'Mary didn't want to come, but I felt it would do her good to be among friends tonight,' Eamonn Doran said over and over again as each of the men embraced Cahill's sister. The little knot of bereaved and sympathisers were in the centre of the almost empty bar. Patricia was standing at the table, forgotten in the concerted movement towards the Dorans. Mulligan felt annoyed, believing she was holding back her sympathy, not controlling her loathing for Cahill.

But Cahill's sister read Patricia's reticence differently and moved towards her, extending her arms, certain in her innocence only of friendship and comfort.

'You must be Patricia. Gerry told us all about the great work you have been doing in Africa.'

Patricia's mouth fell open. Misinterpreting the shock on her face, Mary Doran gathered the younger woman in her arms, and was embraced by Patricia in what appeared to be genuine sympathy. They re-seated, moving the Dorans into the centre of their concern, and the wake of memories and praises started. Kennedy detached himself from the edge of the group and joined a black man at the bar. After a few minutes, Mulligan approached them, his anxiety heightening on hearing the stranger's American accent. Was this one of Charamba's UN scholarship gang? Kennedy had seen Mulligan in the mirror and nodded towards his reflection as he reached the bar. 'John, you remember Jack Clay?'

The American diplomat extended his hand and said, 'the man from Nairobi,' pre-empting Mulligan. Holding Mulligan's hand he added, 'Sorry about your senator.' Then, leaning his face into Mulligan's, he whispered, 'What the hell did Cahill do to them all? They've gone to ground. Nkomo, Charamba, Mugabe. The whole shooting gallery. Out of sight.'

Mulligan shrugged. 'Jack, I'm sure I don't quite understand what you are getting at?'

The American added impatiently.

'Word is that Cahill managed to piss off a whole lot of people in his few days here. And it seems as if you are after blowing whatever slim chance we had of getting on the right side of Prime Minister Robert Mugabe.'

Epilogue

As stated on the title page verso, this is a work of fiction and, except in the case of historical fact, names, characters, organisations, places or events are either the product of the author's imagination or are used fictitiously. Any resemblance of fictitious characters to actual persons, living or dead, is purely coincidental. This epilogue is not fiction.

Joshua Nkomo was initially included in the Mugabe cabinet, but in 1982 tensions between the two men and their supporters heightened and Nkomo was accused of plotting against Mugabe. Guerrillas loyal to Nkomo and ZAPU started to drift back into the bush. Robert Mugabe's government forces, including the North Korean- trained Fifth Brigade, were unleashed on Joshua Nkomo's homeland, Matabeleland, and tens of thousands of civilians were killed in what has become known as the bloodiest time in Rhodesian-Zimbabwean history. These events paved the way for Mugabe's supremacy and the establishment of a one-party state.

End

Plassey Publishing Ltd